5-Minute Fairy Tales

Louis Weber, C.E.O.
Publications International, Ltd.
7373 North Cicero Avenue
Lincolnwood, Illinois 60712

www.pubint.com

Manufactured in China.

8 7 6 5 4 3 2 1

ISBN: 0-7853-3506-4

5-Minute
Fairy Tales

Cover illustrated by Jane Maday
Cover border illustrated by Wendy Edelson

Publications International, Ltd.

Contents

Contents

Contents

Snow White

Illustrated by Burgundy Nilles
Adapted by Jane Jerrard

Long ago in a far-off land, a princess was born with hair as black as night, skin as white as snow, and lips the color of rubies. She was called Snow White.

As the princess grew, she became more beautiful every year. Her stepmother, the queen, was also very beautiful. The queen was so vain, she had a magical mirror made. Every day she looked into the mirror and asked, "Mirror, mirror on the wall, who's the fairest of us all?"

Then the mirror would answer, "You, my queen, are fairest."

And the queen was pleased.

When Snow White grew to be a young maiden, the queen asked, "Mirror, mirror on the wall, who's the fairest of us all?"

The mirror replied, "You, my queen, may lovely be, but Snow White is fairer still than thee."

The queen was very angry. She could not stand to have anyone be prettier than herself. She called a woodsman and ordered him to take Snow White away and kill her.

The man, fearing for his own life, took the girl deep into the forest but could not bring himself to carry out the order. Instead, he left Snow White there alone.

Snow White had never been all by herself in the woods before. Around her were strange noises and scary shadows. She was so scared, she began to run. Tree branches caught at her black hair as she ran through the forest.

Snow White ran as fast as she could, until she came to a little clearing among the trees. There she saw a small cottage with a red roof.

"Maybe someone here will be able to help me," sighed Snow White with relief. She knocked and knocked on the front door. When no one answered, Snow White went inside.

There she found a tiny little table set with seven plates. Snow White was very hungry after being in the woods, so she nibbled a few bites of food from each of the little plates.

After her snack, Snow White found a little bedroom with seven tiny beds. Suddenly Snow White realized she was very, very sleepy.

"I'll just take a little nap," she yawned. She crawled into a bed and was soon fast asleep.

In this cottage lived seven dwarfs. Soon after Snow White fell asleep, the dwarfs came back from work. They quickly discovered that someone was in their house.

Soon the dwarfs saw the beautiful young maiden in their bedroom. When Snow White awoke, she was happy to meet her seven new friends. She told them about the evil queen.

The seven dwarfs felt sorry for Snow White and asked her to stay. She took care of the cottage, and the dwarfs gave her food, friendship, and shelter in return. Snow White was happy living with the dwarfs. She came to love them all so much that she forgot about the evil queen who was so jealous of her beauty.

The evil queen knew that Snow White had not perished in the woods and decided to kill the girl herself. The queen disguised herself as an ugly old woman and searched the woods for Snow White.

One day the evil queen found the dwarfs' cottage. She called out, "Pretty belts for sale!"

Snow White opened the door to the ugly old woman. Snow White tried on one of the lovely belts. The queen pulled the belt so tight around the girl's waist that she fell down as if she were dead. The queen threw off her old woman's costume and shouted, "I will always be the fairest of all!"

When the dwarfs returned home that day, they found Snow White lying in their house. "Poor Snow White!" they cried. Right away they saw that the girl's belt was too tight and cut it off with a knife. She began to breathe again and told them what had happened.

The dwarfs realized that the old woman must have been the evil queen, and they told Snow White to be careful.

"Above all," said the oldest dwarf, "you must never, never open the door for anyone."

Meanwhile, the queen arrived at her castle and asked, "Mirror, mirror on the wall, who's the fairest of us all?"

When the mirror answered that Snow White was still the fairest, the queen vowed that Snow White must die. She set out for the dwarfs' cottage in a new disguise. This time she went to the window of the cottage.

The old woman offered to sell Snow White a lovely comb. Snow White took the comb through the window and put it in her hair. She sank to the ground right where she stood. The comb was poisoned.

It was not long before the dwarfs came home. They saw at once what had happened and quickly removed the comb from Snow White's hair. Then the dwarfs warned her again.

"Snow White, you must never, never open the door or the window for anyone!" said the littlest dwarf.

Back at the castle, the evil queen learned that the princess still lived. She was furious. "I must be rid of Snow White forever!" she cried.

The queen used all her evil magic to make a poisoned apple. Then the queen thought of another disguise. She dressed herself as a poor woman selling fruit and went once more to see Snow White.

This time Snow White was in the garden when the evil queen arrived. The dwarfs had never said anything about talking to strangers outside.

The queen offered the girl the apple, and it looked so delicious that Snow White could not resist it. Snow White bit into the fruit. She instantly fell down as if dead.

When the queen returned to the castle, her mirror told her at last, "Queen, thou art fairest of us all!"

The dwarfs could not wake Snow White, but she looked as healthy and as pretty as if she were comfortably sleeping. They laid her in a glass case so they could watch over her.

One day a prince was hunting in the woods. He came upon Snow White lying in the glass case and asked the dwarfs who she was.

"She is our dear Snow White, put to sleep by the spell of an evil queen," replied one dwarf sadly.

The prince gazed into the glass case. "This is the most beautiful princess I have ever seen," he said. Instantly the prince fell deeply in love.

The prince opened the glass case. As he lifted her up, Snow White slowly opened her eyes and looked at the prince!

When the dwarfs learned that Snow White was alive, they danced with joy and happily agreed that she should marry the handsome prince.

As for the queen, her hatred made her so ugly that she could no longer bear to look in her mirror.

Puss in Boots

Illustrated by Susan Spellman
Adapted by Sarah Toast

Once there was a poor miller who had three sons and very little else. When the old miller died, he left his mill to the eldest son. He left his trustworthy donkey to the middle son. The youngest son got the cat.

The youngest son was upset over his poor share. "My older brothers can work together to earn a living," he said, "but Puss and I will surely die of hunger."

The cat overheard the boy. "Don't worry," said Puss. "Just give me a sack and a good pair of boots so I can walk through the mud and brush, and you'll see that I can be a great help to you."

The boy did what the cat asked. When Puss got his boots, he pulled them on and strutted around.

Then Puss put his new sack over his shoulder and walked to the edge of the woods, where many rabbits lived.

Puss picked tender grass and fresh thistles and put them in the sack. Then he lay down as if he were dead and waited.

A plump, young rabbit soon hopped along and smelled the fresh thistles. He crawled into the bag to eat. Puss jumped up and closed the bag. He brought the rabbit to the king.

Puss was led into the king's throne room. He bowed and said, "Sire, I bring you this gift from my kind master, the duke of Carabas." The king did not know that Puss had just made up this name for the boy.

"Tell your master," said the king, "that I thank him and accept his gift with pleasure." With that, Puss went on his way.

The next day Puss caught two partridges to present to the king. The king was pleased and said, "Thank your generous master, the duke of Carabas. He is most kind."

For many weeks, Puss brought various gifts to the king. The king began to wonder about this mysterious duke of Carabas.

One day Puss found out that the king was taking his daughter for a drive along the river. Puss said to his master, "Go down to the river, take off your clothes, and get in. Leave the rest to me."

The boy did as he was told. Then Puss hid the clothes under a big stone. When the king's coach came along, Puss ran into the road and cried out, "Help! Help! My master, the duke of Carabas, is drowning."

The king ordered that his guards rescue the duke. The princess watched the guards pull the boy from the river.

Puss told the king that horrible robbers had stolen all his master's clothes and had thrown him in the river to drown.

The king wanted to help. He ordered one of his guards to ride back to the palace and bring the duke a dry set of clothes.

Dressed in a fine suit of clothes, the boy did indeed look like a duke. The princess thought he looked handsome. When the duke of Carabas looked at her, the princess smiled back. The king asked the duke to ride with them.

Meanwhile, Puss went ahead of the royal carriage to carry out his plan. He spoke to the farmhands cutting hay in a field. "When the king comes along, you must tell him that this field belongs to the duke of Carabas. If you don't, the ogre who lives in the castle on the hill will chop you into tiny pieces!"

Sure enough, when the king drove up he asked the farmhands who owned the land.

"The duke of Carabas!" they answered.

A little farther down the road, when the king asked more farmhands who owned the land they were working, they all answered the same thing, "The duke of Carabas!" And so it went.

Everywhere the king asked, he was told that the land belonged to the duke of Carabas. The king was amazed at how much land the duke owned and how wealthy he was.

"The duke of Carabas," the king thought. "Now that is a name I surely intend to remember."

The princess, who was sitting beside the duke in the carriage, was not paying much attention to the duke's wealth. She gazed into his eyes during the entire journey.

The duke and the princess talked and talked. By now the princess felt she loved the duke. He in turn fell in love with the princess.

While the princess and the duke talked and got to know one another, Puss went ahead to the ogre's castle.

He was a very rich ogre. He owned all the surrounding land and had heaps of treasure hidden away inside his castle.

The horrible ogre was also said to have special powers. He could change into any animal at all. But Puss had a plan and would ask to see the ogre's powers for himself.

When Puss got to the castle, he asked to see the ogre. Then Puss boldly said, "I have heard of your powers to change yourself into any animal at all, even a lion or an elephant!"

"It is true," roared the ogre as he changed into a fearsome lion.

Puss leaped up onto a cupboard. He jumped down when the ogre turned himself back into an ogre.

Puss told the ogre that he was very frightened. Then he said, "I have heard that you can also change yourself into a very tiny animal, even a mouse. But that's impossible!"

"What? Impossible?!" roared the ogre. "Not impossible for me!" In the blink of an eye, he changed himself into a mouse.

Puss wasted no time. He pounced on the mouse and ate it. As the mouse was gone, so was the ogre.

Meanwhile, the king's coach had arrived at the castle. Puss ran out to welcome the king and the princess. Puss bowed and said, "Welcome to the castle of the duke of Carabas!"

"Don't tell me this fine castle is yours, dear duke!" exclaimed the king.

The duke merely smiled and led the king and the princess into the great hall. The king, the princess, the duke, and Puss enjoyed a splendid feast. Then the king offered the charming duke his lovely daughter's hand in marriage.

The duke and the princess were married that day. As for clever Puss, he lived a life of ease in the castle ever after.

Rapunzel

Illustrated by Barbara Lanza
Adapted by Lisa Harkrader

There was once a poor man and woman who lived in a tiny cottage in the woods. Every year they worked hard tending their garden, but their land was small, and the soil was rocky. They could grow barely enough food to feed themselves.

Their cottage stood next to a witch's castle. The castle's grounds were filled with lush gardens and orchards. The garden grew more food than the witch could eat, and every year the man and woman watched the vegetables rot on the vines.

One day the man could stand it no longer. He crept over the garden wall and filled his sack with peas and squash, potatoes and corn.

Just then a voice called, "Drop those vegetables!"

The man turned and saw the witch looming over him.

"You won't get away with stealing from me! When your first child is born, you must give the baby to me," said the witch.

A year went by, and a daughter was born to the man and his wife. They named her Rapunzel and kept her hidden in the cottage. The man read stories and played games with her. The woman made up lullabies and sang them to her night and day.

The witch watched the cottage from her castle. One day she heard the woman singing.

"Lullabies?" snarled the witch. The witch crept up to the cottage and peeked in the window. There she saw the baby Rapunzel. "A child!" shrieked the witch.

Before the man or woman could stop her, the witch snatched Rapunzel from her cradle.

The witch carried Rapunzel to her castle and locked her inside. The chambers were dark and lonely, but as the years went by Rapunzel grew into a lovely girl, well-mannered and bright.

Rapunzel was so bright, she began asking questions.

"Why are the windows covered so we can't see out?" asked Rapunzel. "What is beyond that big door?"

The witch would not reply, but she knew that Rapunzel would try to find her own answers to these questions. So she led Rapunzel to a tower deep in the woods. The tower had no doors and no stairs. The only opening was one small window high above the ground. The witch locked Rapunzel inside.

Each morning the witch brought food to Rapunzel. She called up, "Rapunzel, Rapunzel! Let down your hair."

Rapunzel would bend her head out the window and let her hair tumble down. It was so long it reached the ground, and so strong the witch was able to climb the shiny locks up to the window.

Rapunzel was very lonely in the tower. She sang familiar lullabies to pass the time.

One day a prince from a nearby kingdom heard Rapunzel singing and followed her voice to the tower.

The prince realized that the song was coming from inside, but he could not find a way in. He listened to the enchanting music, hoping to see whose voice filled the woods with song.

Then he saw the witch creeping through the woods. The prince heard her call out, "Rapunzel, Rapunzel! Let down your hair."

The prince watched in amazement as the shiny, golden locks dropped to the ground. "She is by far the most beautiful creature on earth," he said.

The prince waited until the witch was gone. Then, he called out, "Rapunzel, Rapunzel! Let down your hair."

Rapunzel let down her hair, expecting to see the witch again. When the prince climbed into view, Rapunzel gasped.

"Don't be afraid," said the prince. "I heard your beautiful lullabies and wanted to meet you."

The prince was the most handsome thing Rapunzel had ever seen. The two fell in love immediately.

Rapunzel knew that with the prince's help she could leave the tower. The prince climbed down Rapunzel's hair then caught her as she leaped to freedom. They set off for the prince's kingdom.

They passed a small cottage, and Rapunzel heard a familiar lullaby. They saw an old man and woman inside the cottage.

"Your songs are lovely," Rapunzel told the woman.

"I sang them to my daughter, Rapunzel," said the woman.

Rapunzel hugged the man and woman. "I'm Rapunzel," she said. "I've escaped from the witch."

Rapunzel sang the lullabies in a full, joyful voice. "These songs have led me back to you," said Rapunzel.

Goldilocks and the Three Bears

Illustrated by Burgandy Nilles
Adapted by Sarah Toast

Once upon a time there was a bear family who lived in a lovely house in the woods. There was a great big Papa Bear, a middle-size Mama Bear, and a wee Baby Bear.

They each had a chair to sit in: a great big chair for Papa Bear, a middle-size chair for Mama Bear, and a wee chair for Baby Bear.

And they each had
a bed to sleep in that
was just the right size.

Every morning for
breakfast they each ate a
heaping bowl of tasty
porridge: a great big
bowl for Papa Bear, a
middle-size bowl for
Mama Bear, and a wee
bowl for Baby Bear.

One morning the
porridge was much too
hot to eat. The three
bears went for a walk while the porridge was cooling. Mama
Bear took her basket so she could gather sweet blackberries
to stir into the porridge.

The three bears did not lock their door when they went out because they were very trusting bears who lived deep in the quiet forest. They never thought that anyone would enter their house while they were gone.

While the three bears were out walking, a little girl named Goldilocks passed by their lovely little house. Goldilocks had been out walking since early in the morning. She had not eaten any breakfast before she left home, and the three bears' porridge smelled very good to her.

Goldilocks looked in the window and saw the bowls of hot porridge sitting on the table. She looked around and did not see anyone inside. Since no one was home, Goldilocks pushed open the door and walked into the three bears' house!

She saw three sets of slippers laid out for the next morning. One pair of slippers was for someone with great big feet. Goldilocks saw a second pair of slippers for middle-size feet. Another pair was for somebody with wee feet.

Goldilocks looked and saw three jars of honey. Every jar was a different size, too. The whole house, Goldilocks noticed, was filled with three of just about everything in three different sizes! One was a great big thing, another was middle-size, and the third was always a wee thing.

This house must belong to a family of three, Goldilocks guessed. She thought they would not mind if she helped herself to just one little bit of the three bowls of porridge set out on the table.

Goldilocks went right over to the table and began helping herself to the porridge. First she sampled the porridge in the great big bowl. "Ouch!" said Goldilocks, "This porridge is far too hot!"

Since Goldilocks was very hungry, she could not wait for the porridge to cool. So she decided to taste the porridge in the middle-size bowl. "Oh no," she said, making a face. "This porridge is much too cold."

Then Goldilocks tasted the porridge in the wee bowl. It was just right. It was so good she ate it all up.

When Goldilocks finished the porridge, she wandered into the next room, where she saw three chairs.

First Goldilocks sat in the great big chair. "This chair is too hard," she said. Next she sat in the middle-size chair. "And this chair is too soft," complained Goldilocks. Finally she sat in the wee chair. "This chair is just right," said Goldilocks. Goldilocks sat there in the wee chair, enjoying the peace and quiet, when suddenly the little chair broke all to pieces.

Goldilocks picked herself up off the floor and put the pieces of the wee chair back together as best she could. Then she went upstairs.

At the top of the stairs, Goldilocks found the bedroom. First she lay on the great big bed. "This bed is too hard," said Goldilocks. Then she lay on the middle-size bed. "This bed is much too soft," she complained.

Goldilocks walked over to the wee bed and lay down on it. "This bed is just right," said Goldilocks. She snuggled under the covers and in no time was fast asleep.

By now the three bears thought their porridge would be cool enough to eat, so they returned home. The bears entered the house. They could not wait to taste their porridge with the blackberries Mama Bear had picked.

Papa Bear saw the spoons standing in the three bowls of porridge. "Someone has been tasting my porridge," Papa Bear growled.

Mama Bear looked at her bowl and said, "Someone's been tasting my porridge!"

Then Baby Bear saw that his wee bowl was empty. "Look! Someone has been tasting my porridge and has eaten it all up!" he cried.

Now the three bears knew that someone had been inside their house. They wondered if that someone was still there. The bears went into the next room to look around.

Papa Bear went up to his great big chair and said, "Someone has been sitting in my chair."

Mama Bear saw her chair. "Someone has been sitting in my chair!"

Then Baby Bear looked at his own wee chair. He cried out, "Someone has been sitting in my chair, and now it's broken!"

The three bears hurried upstairs to their bedroom. Papa Bear noticed right away that his bedcovers were rumpled. "Someone has been lying on my bed," he growled in his great big voice.

Mama Bear saw that her pillows and quilts were a mess. "Someone has been lying on my bed, too," she said in her middle-size voice.

While Mama Bear and Papa Bear were looking at their beds, Baby Bear walked over to his wee bed. He cried out in his wee voice, "Someone has been sleeping in my bed, and here she is!" He leaned over to touch the sleeping girl to see if she was real.

Goldilocks awoke with a start. She saw the three bears standing beside the bed. She was so scared that she tumbled out of the bed. She ran out of the room and down the stairs as fast as she could.

The three bears never saw Goldilocks again, and that was just fine with them.

Cinderella

Illustrated by Susan Spellman
Adapted by Jane Jerrard

Once upon a time, there was a young girl who was very kind and beautiful. The girl had a mean stepmother. The stepmother and her two nasty daughters treated the girl as a servant. They made her scrub the floors and wash the dishes and pick up after them. She was called Cinderella because at the end of the day she would be covered with dark cinders from the hearth.

Cinderella was always cheerful and polite. Her kindness made her even more beautiful. Cinderella's stepmother and stepsisters spent their days preening in front of a mirror and talking about which one of them would marry the handsome prince of the kingdom.

Cinderella was too busy with her stepsister's tasks to think about the prince.

One day something exciting arrived. It was an invitation to the prince's ball! All the fine people in the kingdom were invited, and the sisters worried about what to wear. As they prepared for the ball, they began to treat Cinderella even more cruelly than before.

Cinderella sewed and ironed for days. She was treated as if she was their personal servant. The poor girl was not allowed to go to the ball herself. Besides, she did not have a dress nice enough for the ball.

Finally the night arrived. As Cinderella helped her younger stepsister into her gown, the cruel girl asked, "Cinderella, why don't you come with us to the ball and dance with the prince?"

The stepmother and her daughters laughed at the thought of dirty, barefoot Cinderella dancing with the handsome prince. Saddened, Cinderella looked down at the floor. As Cinderella's stepmother and stepsisters climbed into their coach and rode off to the ball, Cinderella began to cry.

"Why must I stay at home and sweep while everyone else goes to the ball?" cried Cinderella.

Cinderella wanted to put on a fine dress and dance in the palace hall. Most of all, she wanted to catch a glimpse of the handsome prince. Maybe he would ask her to dance!

Suddenly, a beautiful fairy appeared. It was Cinderella's fairy godmother! "What is wrong, dear Cinderella?" asked the fairy godmother. The fairy had secretly watched over Cinderella's hard life, and this was the first time she had ever seen the girl cry.

Cinderella explained that she wanted very much to go to the ball to meet the prince.

"So you shall go, Cinderella," said the fairy godmother. "For you have always been good."

Cinderella could not believe her ears. "But I have no coach to take me there," she said.

"Not to worry, my dear," replied Cinderella's fairy godmother. With her magic, she turned a pumpkin into a handsome coach.

"But who will drive the coach?" she asked.

Cinderella's fairy godmother found six mice and turned them into six fine horses, ready to pull Cinderella's carriage. All that was missing was a driver. A white rat was magically turned into the quickest driver in the land!

"Now you can go to the ball!" said the fairy godmother.

"But my clothes. . . ," whispered Cinderella. "I cannot go to the fancy ball in dirty rags!"

With one touch of her wand, her fairy godmother turned Cinderella's old dress into a lovely gown trimmed in gold. She gave the girl a pair of glass slippers that fit just right!

"Thank you so much, fairy godmother!" cried Cinderella.

With that, her handsome footman helped Cinderella into the magical pumpkin coach. Cinderella was so excited. She could not believe that she was not dreaming a wonderful dream.

"Be home before midnight, Cinderella," she called. "My magic will disappear when the clock strikes twelve!"

"I won't be late. Thank you!" Cinderella waved out the window of her coach.

Off she rode to the ball. When the carriage arrived at the palace, Cinderella saw a great gold clock at the top of one of the towers.

"Good," she sighed. "Now I surely won't be late."

Cinderella stepped out of her coach and climbed the stairs to the palace. When she appeared in the doorway, everyone at the ball turned to look at her. Cinderella was far more beautiful than any of the princesses in attendance.

The prince was busy greeting his guests when he saw Cinderella. He took one look at her and fell in love. Aside from being lovely, Cinderella was also charming and sweet. As the prince and Cinderella danced, all the people smiled and watched. No one recognized her.

Cinderella discovered that the handsome prince was also very kind. She was so happy, she forgot the time. The clock was striking the midnight hour when Cinderella remembered the promise she had made to her fairy godmother. Cinderella dashed out of the ballroom without a word to the prince, leaving him and the rest of the guests astonished!

Cinderella was in such a hurry that she left one of her glass slippers behind.

Cinderella's dress was transformed back into her tattered rags. She ran as fast as she could so that no one would recognize her.

The prince ran after Cinderella, but she was already gone. He wanted to call out to her, but she never told him her name! The prince spied the glass slipper on the palace steps. He vowed to find the glass slipper's mysterious owner.

Cinderella ran home dressed in rags. Her coach had turned into a pumpkin, and the mice and the rat had run away. All she had left was the other glass slipper.

The next day everyone could talk of nothing but the ball and the beautiful stranger who stole the prince's heart.

"This glass slipper is all I have," said the prince. "I must use it to find her." That very day he began to search for the maiden who could wear the delicate slipper.

The prince arrived at the house where Cinderella lived. The stepsisters both tried on the slipper, but neither could put it on.

Cinderella had been watching from beside the fire. She asked softly, "May I please try to put on the slipper?"

Her stepmother and stepsisters laughed and told her not to waste the prince's precious time.

The prince knelt and held out the glass slipper for Cinderella. Her foot slipped into it with ease! Cinderella pulled the other glass slipper from her apron pocket and put it on, too.

Cinderella went back to the palace with the prince. He was so overcome with love and joy that they were married that very day!

Vasilissa and the Magic Doll

Illustrated by Nan Brooks
Adapted by Sarah Toast

Long ago, in far-away Russia, there lived a merchant and his wife. They had a daughter named Vasilissa. Vasilissa was young when her mother became ill.

"Beloved daughter," Vasilissa's mother said, "I am dying, but do not be sad. I have made you a doll that you must keep with you always. Do not tell anyone about her."

Vasilissa took the doll and slipped it into her pocket.

"Whenever you are sad or afraid," said her mother, "give the doll a bit to eat and drink. Then tell her your troubles. She will tell you what to do."

Vasilissa kissed her mother.

"Bless you, child, and do not cry," said her mother. "I will always be with you." Then she closed her eyes.

Vasilissa tried not to cry. She reached for her doll. Vasilissa gave the doll a tiny piece of bread and a drop of milk. She whispered, "I am so sad that my mother has died and left me."

The doll's eyes seemed to shine, and Vasilissa heard a voice saying, "Do not cry, little Vasilissa. Go to sleep. The morning is wiser than the evening." Vasilissa lay down in her bed and slept.

One day, Vasilissa's father returned from a trip with a new wife. She had two daughters a few years older than Vasilissa. Her daughters were jealous of Vasilissa's beauty, and Vasilissa's new stepmother was as cruel as Vasilissa was kind.

The stepmother and her daughters made Vasilissa do all the hard work around the house while they sat lazily about. They spoke only hurtful words to the child.

Every night, Vasilissa took her doll from her pocket. She fed the doll bits of food she saved. She whispered to the doll all her troubles. The doll's eyes would shine, and she would speak words of comfort to Vasilissa.

Over the years, Vasilissa grew in beauty, and young men of the village wanted to marry her. Her stepmother was furious.

"The youngest daughter of the house shall not marry before the elder daughters!" she screamed and sent the suitors away.

Vasilissa's father had to go far away to buy goods. The cruel stepmother had a plan to get rid of Vasilissa. She moved the family to a cottage at the edge of a dark forest. In the forest there lived a witch called Baba Yaga.

One evening, the stepmother went to bed and left only one candle burning. Following her mother's instructions, the eldest stepsister put out the candle. The house was in total darkness.

The second stepsister cried out, "What shall we do? There is no light! Vasilissa, you must go to Baba Yaga's hut to fetch some light!" Then the two stepsisters pushed Vasilissa out the door into the dark night.

Vasilissa sat down and fed her doll bits of food. Then she said, "I am frightened! I need your help!"

The doll said, "Do not fear. I will keep you from harm."

Vasilissa walked through the woods until the path ended. In front of her was Baba Yaga's hut perched on chicken legs. On the gate to the hut stood animal skulls.

Vasilissa saw the skulls on the fence light up, casting an eerie glow. She heard Baba Yaga cry out a hideous scream.

Baba Yaga approached Vasilissa and told her she must work for the light she came looking for. The witch ordered Vasilissa to bring her all the food from the oven. Baba Yaga ate enough for three people, but she gave Vasilissa only a bit of bread and meat to eat. Vasilissa saved some food in her pocket.

Baba Yaga told Vasilissa that the next day she would have to scrub the floors, do the washing, cook the witch's supper, and clean an entire bushel of wheat while Baba Yaga was gone, or she would never go home again. When Baba Yaga fell asleep, Vasilissa took her doll out and told her of Baba Yaga's harsh demands.

The doll said, "Go to sleep. You have nothing to worry about."

When Vasilissa awoke the next morning, Baba Yaga was already gone. Vasilissa found that her tasks had already been done. Vasilissa thanked her doll and rested. At the end of the day, she set the table for the witch's supper.

When Baba Yaga returned, she was disappointed that Vasilissa was able to finish her tasks. Baba Yaga ate her supper and said sharply, "Why don't you talk to me?"

"I do not dare," said Vasilissa.

"Tell me how you were able to finish your tasks," demanded Baba Yaga.

Vasilissa could not tell her about the doll, but she wished to be truthful. She said, "My dead mother's blessing helped me."

The witch screamed, "Blessings! We'll have no blessings in this house! Get out now!"

Vasilissa ran as fast as she could. As she ran, she grabbed a glowing skull from the fence for light. She could not disappoint her stepsisters by not bringing home light.

When she reached the edge of the woods, Vasilissa saw that everything was as she had left it, but nobody was home.

The next day, Vasilissa's father came back from his journey. When Vasilissa saw her father, she wept tears of joy. Vasilissa kept her doll and her mother's blessing with her always.

The Honest Woodcutter

Illustrated by Tammie Speer Lyon
Adapted by Jennifer Boudart

There once was a woodcutter who lived with his wife and two children in a forest far from town. The woodcutter built his home with logs that he cut himself. The house was not big or fancy, but it was warm and dry. The family was not rich, but they were happy and lived comfortably.

One morning at breakfast, the family joked about what their lives would be like if they had lots of money. The woodcutter wished for a bigger house, his wife dreamed of eating from fine china plates, and the children imagined playing with all sorts of wonderful toys.

After breakfast, the woodcutter grabbed his ax and headed to work. His family waved good-bye to him as he walked deep into the forest. The woodcutter worked in the oldest part of the forest, where the trees were the tallest, thickest, and hardest.

But the trees were no problem for the woodcutter. He was the best around. He simply sharpened his trusty old ax and went to work.

Soon woodchips flew through the air, and the forest echoed with the sound of the woodcutter's ax chopping. It was like beautiful music. These were days that made the woodcutter the happiest.

A little squirrel happened to be nearby collecting nuts and heard the noise. The squirrel went to investigate and was amazed by how quickly the woodcutter chopped. She sat on a large pile of logs that the woodcutter had chopped earlier that morning. The woodcutter did not notice that the squirrel was sitting there.

"You're the fastest woodcutter I've ever seen," said the squirrel in amazement.

The woodcutter thought only about cutting more wood so he could give his family all the things they wanted.

Every day the trusty woodcutter worked until noon then took a short break. The woodcutter always wanted to get back to work. The more he worked, the better off his family would be.

All of his work made the woodcutter very thirsty. He walked quickly to get a drink.

The woodcutter tripped over a rock. When he fell, his ax slipped out of his hands and landed in the river.

The woodcutter ran to the edge of the water. He looked into the river to find his ax, but it was gone.

Without his ax, the woodcutter could not chop wood. And without wood, he could not buy the things his family wanted.

"What am I going to do?" said the woodcutter.

Suddenly the river made a noise. The woodcutter saw the water rising. It grew arms and a head, and it started to talk!

"I am the water sprite, a fairy of this river. Why are you so sad?" said the water sprite.

The woodcutter told him what had happened.

The water sprite said, "Don't worry. I'll find your ax." In an instant the sprite was gone, and the river began to swirl and foam.

After a few moments, the water sprite appeared again. This time the sprite smiled and held something in his watery hands. "Is this your ax?" he asked the woodcutter. "I found it in the rocks at the bottom of the river."

The woodcutter looked at the ax. Whoever owned it was rich indeed. The ax was made of pure silver! The woodcutter thought about taking it, but it did not belong to him. Saying the ax was his would be wrong.

"I cannot take this ax. It is not mine," he said.

The water sprite tossed the silver ax on the ground and said, "Very well, I'll look for your ax again." Once again the sprite left to look for the woodcutter's ax. When the he returned, he held an ax that was even more magnificent than the first one. It was made of solid gold!

The woodcutter held the gold ax for a moment. This ax could make him very rich. But the woodcutter gave the ax back.

"This is a fine ax," he explained. "But this ax is not mine. Someone must be looking for it and misses it."

The water sprite said, "Let me look for it once more." When he returned, he held another ax. This ax was not shiny at all, and the handle was worn from use.

The woodcutter smiled and said, "Ah yes! This is my ax."

"Your ax is not worth much, but your honesty is. The silver and gold axes belong to me. I want you to take them as a gift for telling the truth."

The woodcutter was very excited to have all three axes. He thanked the water sprite and left the forest early that day.

Instead of going straight home, the woodcutter went into town to go shopping. He could not wait to get to the store. He was sure that the store owner would buy the gold and silver axes from him.

When the woodcutter arrived, he handed the fine axes to the store owner. The owner looked them over carefully and

finally said, "These are the best axes that I have ever seen. I will gladly buy them."

The store owner was very generous. He gave the woodcutter a large sack of gold coins! The woodcutter bought an armful of beautiful flowers for his wife.

The woodcutter bought fine china plates for his wife, too. He also bought a big bag of toys for his children. The woodcutter had lots of gold left over and carried it all back home.

His wife and children were surprised that the woodcutter was home so early. They ran from the house to meet him. When the woodcutter's wife saw the china plates and the flowers, she was so happy that tears came to her eyes. When the children saw the big bag filled with toys, they squealed with joy.

The woodcutter told his family all that had happened to him during the day and all about the amazing water sprite.

That night, as he and his wife were putting the children to bed, his son looked up at him and asked, "Why did the water sprite give you all three axes?"

Then the woodcutter's daughter said, "Because you told the truth, right?"

"That's right," said the honest woodcutter. "Because I told the truth."

Jack and the Beanstalk

Illustrated by Susan Spellman
Adapted by Jane Jerrard

There was once a poor widow who lived with her son, Jack, far out in the country. Jack was good-natured but lazy. When at last there was no money left to buy food, Jack's mother told him to take the dairy cow to market and sell her for a good price.

On his way to market, Jack met a strange man who asked him where he was going with the cow.

"I'm going to market to sell her," he said.

"I will give you these five magic beans for the cow," said the strange man.

Jack thought this was a good bargain, so he traded the cow for five beans.

Jack hurried home and said, "Look at the five beans I got for the cow!"

"You foolish, lazy boy!" cried his mother angrily. "Now we will go hungry." She threw all the beans out the window, and she and Jack went to bed without any supper.

When Jack awoke early the next morning, he noticed an odd shadow across his window. He ran outside to see that a huge beanstalk had sprung up during the night. It grew so high he could not see the top.

Jack was curious and decided to climb up the beanstalk. He climbed for hours. When he finally reached the top, he saw a great castle in the clouds.

The magnificent castle looked as if it were a vision in a dream. Jack knew from his tired arms and legs that he had not just dreamed his long climb. He rubbed his eyes to make sure he was not seeing things.

As he got closer to the castle, Jack met a beautiful fairy. She told Jack that the giant who lived in the castle had killed Jack's father long ago and had stolen all his gold. The tiny fairy said that he should take back what was rightfully his, and then she disappeared.

When Jack reached the steps, he asked the giant's huge wife for some supper.

"If you stay here, the giant will have you for supper," she said. But Jack was so hungry that he did not care.

The woman gave in and fixed Jack a good supper. Soon they heard the thump, thump of heavy footsteps. Just as the giant entered the room, his wife hid Jack in the oven.

The giant sniffed the air and roared, "Fee-fi-fo-fum! I smell the blood of an Englishman!"

"It's just your supper," said his wife.

The giant ate his huge supper in one huge swallow. Then he roared, "Fetch my gold coins!"

The woman brought in bags of gold coins that had belonged to Jack's father. The giant fell fast asleep counting the money.

Jack took a bag of gold and ran back to the beanstalk. He threw the bag down to his mother's garden and climbed down as fast as he could. Jack's mother was overcome with joy when gold coins rained down. They could now take care of their needs for awhile. But then one day the gold ran out.

Jack disguised himself and went up the beanstalk again. He wanted more of his father's gold.

When Jack returned to the castle, very tired and hungry, the giant's wife did not want to help him.

"The last boy I helped stole a bag of my husband's gold," she said.

But Jack was so polite that she finally let him in and gave him a drink of water.

Just then the giant's footsteps shook the floor. Jack barely had time to hide in the oven before the giant entered the kitchen and roared angrily, "Fee-fi-fo-fum, I smell the blood of an Englishman!"

"Don't be silly," said the giant's wife.

The giant ate his supper and then he told his wife to bring him his hen.

Jack heard the giant shout, "Lay!" When he peeked through a hole in the oven, he saw the hen lay a perfect golden egg. After he told the hen to lay three golden eggs, the giant fell asleep.

Jack leaped out of the oven, snatched the hen, and ran. When Jack reached the beanstalk, he began to climb down quickly. He took the wonderful hen to his mother. The hen laid a golden egg on command every time. With the golden eggs, Jack and his mother were able to fix up their cottage, and there was always plenty to eat.

After a while, however, Jack decided to climb back up the beanstalk. Jack sneaked back into the castle and hid in a large pot.

The giant sniffed the air and said, "Fee-fi-fo-fum!" His wife went over to the oven and looked in, but there was no boy inside.

After the giant ate his supper, he called for his magic harp. His wife quickly brought him his beautiful harp of gold.

The giant told the harp to play. It began to play the most entrancing music Jack had ever heard.

It was not long before the giant was lulled to sleep by the music. When Jack heard the giant snoring, he knew it was safe to climb out of the pot. He grabbed the giant's harp and started to run away with it.

"Master! Master!" the harp cried. The giant awoke with a start. Jack jumped off the table, the harp in his arms, just as the giant made a grab for him. Jack tightly held onto the harp and ran for his life.

Jack could hear the huge thump, thump of the giant's footsteps closing in behind him. He knew the giant took large steps, so his fear was great. But the angry giant had just finished a filling supper, and that slowed him down enough for Jack to reach the beanstalk ahead of the giant.

Jack clumsily climbed down the beanstalk with the harp, calling out to his mother as he went. "Mother! Bring me the ax!"

The giant was halfway down the beanstalk when Jack reached the ground. Jack took the ax from his mother. With one mighty chop, he cut the beanstalk in two. The giant crashed to the ground and died.

Jack, his mother, the hen, and the harp lived happily ever after.

Twelve Dancing Princesses

Illustrated by Pamela R. Levy
Adapted by Sarah Toast

Long ago there lived a king who had twelve beautiful and clever daughters. The princesses slept in the same room with twelve beds in a row. The king loved his daughters, but he was concerned about what they did each night. The king carefully locked the door of the princesses' room every night, but the next morning he always found the princesses tired and out of sorts. More puzzling still, their silk dancing slippers were worn to shreds.

When the king asked his daughters why they were so tired, the princesses merely said, "Beloved Papa, we have been sleeping peacefully in our beds all night."

The king wanted to find out the truth about his daughters.

So the king issued a proclamation around the kingdom that the first man to solve the mystery of where the princesses went to dance every night would choose a wife from among them. However, anyone who tried to discover the princesses' secret had only three nights to succeed.

It was not long before a prince arrived at the palace to try his luck. The prince was led to a small chamber next to the princesses' bedroom where a door connecting the two rooms was left open. The twelve princesses could not leave without being seen by the prince. The prince accepted a cup of wine offered to him by the princesses. In no time, he was sound asleep in his bed.

When the prince awoke the next morning, the princesses were asleep in their beds. The prince was surprised to see all their worn-out shoes!

The next two nights, the same thing happened. The king was very angry and he banished the prince from the kingdom. Many other princes met the same fate. The king thought he would never find out the mystery of where his daughters danced at night.

One day a poor, wounded soldier came limping along the road. He had just sat down by the side of the road to eat his meager meal of bread and cheese when an old woman appeared all dressed in rags. "Won't you have a bite to eat with me?" said the soldier to the woman. He offered her half of his simple meal.

"Where are you going?" asked the woman.

"I'm going to find work," replied the soldier. "Perhaps I can find out how the princesses wear out their shoes!"

The old woman said, "Listen! Do not drink the wine that the princesses offer you. Take this cloak, for it will make you invisible. Then you can follow the princesses and discover their secret!"

The soldier thanked the old woman and headed at once to the king's palace.

That night, the soldier was led to the room next to the princesses' bedroom. He was offered a cup of wine. The soldier pretended to drink the wine, letting it drip into his scarf. Then he lied down and pretended to sleep.

When the eldest princess heard the soldier's snores, she said, "Make haste. We must get ready for the ball!"

The princesses chattered and laughed as they dressed in their best gowns and jewels and arranged each other's hair. Only the youngest princess felt uneasy. "Something isn't right," she said.

"Don't be a little goose," said the eldest princess fondly. "That soldier is sound asleep. He won't be up until morning!"

When the princesses were ready, they put on their dancing shoes. Then the eldest princess tapped on her bedpost three times. The bed sank into the floor and became a staircase. The eldest princess stepped down into the opening in the floor. One by one, her sisters followed her.

The soldier sprang out of bed and threw on the magic cloak. Then he followed the youngest princess down the long stairway. Because his leg was lame, the soldier stumbled and stepped on the hem of the youngest princess's gown. She shrieked with alarm.

The princesses and the soldier went down many flights of stairs until they came to a forest of silver trees. Then they came across trees of gold and trees of diamonds. The soldier broke off a branch from each kind of tree that they passed.

The princesses hurried to the edge of a beautiful lake. There, twelve princes awaited them in twelve little painted boats. Each princess took the hand of a handsome prince.

The soldier quickly hopped into the boat with the youngest princess and her prince.

On the other side of the lake stood a lovely castle. As the boats approached the castle, a fanfare of trumpets announced the arrival of the twelve dancing princesses and fireworks lit up the sky. The princes and the princesses stepped into the castle, where beautiful music welcomed them. There the princesses danced with their princes for half the night.

Soon the princesses' slippers were worn-out. The princes rowed the twelve princesses back across the lake, and this time the soldier rode with the eldest sister. The princesses bade their princes good-bye and promised to return the next night.

Then the princesses hurried back the way they came. They were so tired that they slowed down at the top of the last set of stairs. The soldier was able to dash ahead of them, throw off his cloak, and jump into his bed.

The princesses got to their room and put their worn and tattered shoes in a row. The eldest princess checked on the soldier to be sure he was asleep and said to her sisters, "We are safe!" With that, all twelve sisters fell fast asleep in their beds.

The soldier wanted to see the forests and the castle again, so he did not reveal what he knew the next day.

The soldier did the same thing for the next two nights. He pretended to sleep and followed the princesses. On the third night, the soldier took a golden cup from the castle to show the king as proof.

The next morning the king sent for the soldier and asked him, "Good soldier, have you discovered where my daughters dance their shoes to shreds every night?"

"Your Highness, I have," said the soldier. "They sneak down a hidden staircase. Then they walk through three enchanted forests to a beautiful lake. There twelve princes take them across the lake to a castle where they dance the night away."

The king could not believe the soldier's story, but then the soldier showed him the golden cup and the branches of silver, gold, and diamonds. The king called his daughters, who admitted the truth.

The king told the soldier that since he solved the mystery he could choose one of the princesses to be his wife.

The soldier had already decided that he liked the eldest princess best. She was clever and spirited, as well as very beautiful. For her part, the princess thought the soldier was clever and kind.

The soldier was given royal garments to wear. He and the eldest princess were married, and all the wedding guests happily danced the night away.

The Frog Prince

Illustrated by Kathy Mitchell
Adapted by Eric Fein

Once upon a time, in a kingdom far away, there lived a king who had many beautiful children. But the most beautiful was his youngest daughter.

In the summer, when the kingdom broiled with heat, the young princess would sit by the edge of a deep, cool well and daydream. And sometimes, she would play with her favorite golden ball. She would toss the ball high up in the air and catch it.

She loved to do that. It made the day go by quickly.

One afternoon, as she was playing with her golden ball, she threw it up into the air a little too high. She ran after it. But before she could catch it, it fell into the well.

The well was much too deep for the princess to get her ball. Were she to climb in, she would not be able to climb back out. The only thing she could do was lean over the side, look into the well, and weep over the loss of her beautiful golden ball.

"What will I do without my lovely golden ball," she cried. "Won't somebody help me?"

She wept for quite some time, until she heard a voice say, "What troubles you, fair young princess?"

The princess looked down into the well and saw a frog sitting amongst the cattails.

"I am crying because my golden ball is lost in the well," the princess told the frog.

The frog said, "Weep no more fair princess, for I shall rescue your golden ball. Though I must know, what you shall give me for performing such a deed."

"Oh, anything you desire," she said.

"What I wish for is your promise that you will love me and have me as your friend and playmate; that you will take me home with you and let me share your food. And at night, you will tuck me into bed with you," said the frog.

"Oh, yes, dear frog. I agree to what you ask," said the princess, but she was lying.

Overjoyed that the princess agreed to his terms, the frog dove under the water and found the golden ball. It was stuck tightly in the mud and he had to work hard to free it.

As soon as the frog set the ball down, the princess snatched it up and took off running.

The poor frog could not keep up with the princess. He called after her, "Wait, princess, wait! You didn't take me! Come back!"

But the princess was halfway home.

That evening, the princess sat down to dinner with the king and queen. The royal family was enjoying their dinner when there came a shout, "Young princess, let me in!"

The princess turned pale. She excused herself from the table and opened the door to let the frog inside.

The frog looked around and said, "My, what a nice home you have. I will enjoy living here." He sniffed the air and said, "Is that beef stew I smell?" Then the frog jumped onto the table.

The king said, "Daughter, why is there a frog at the dinner table?"

The princess explained about how the ball fell into the well and how she had made a promise to the frog if he would return it to her.

"Well, you have made a pledge," said the king, "and it must not be broken."

Sadly, the princess turned to the frog and said, "My dinner is your dinner. My friendship is for you, and my bed is your bed."

"Wonderful," croaked the frog as he began to eat all the food on her plate. His tongue lashed out over and over to grab the food. He had two helpings of everything. The princess lost her appetite watching the frog eat.

"Now I am tired," said the frog. "Take me to your room to sleep on your silken sheets. The first thing I want to see in the morning is your beautiful face."

The princess began to weep, "I cannot go through with this. It is too horrible. I refuse."

"No more weeping. I am tired, take me to bed," said the frog.

The frog's teasing was too much for the princess. "No, you horrible frog." She slammed her palm on the table. The table shook and the frog lost his balance. He fell off the table.

Suddenly, the frog turned into a handsome young prince.

"What is going on here?" asked the princess.

The prince explained, "Dear princess, I am so sorry to have caused you so much pain, but an evil witch turned me into a frog. The only way I could become a prince again was to get a princess angry at me. Because princesses hardly ever lose their temper, I thought I was doomed to live forever as a frog."

"You poor thing," said the princess. "Such a handsome young man, destined for the lonely life of a frog. How horrible!"

In that brief moment, the princess and the prince fell in love. The prince proposed and the princess accepted. The prince and the princess lived a long and happy life together.

The Nightingale

Illustrated by Robin Moro
Adapted by Lisa Harkrader

Many years ago, the emperor of China lived in a palace that was surrounded by beautiful gardens. Visitors came from all over the world to admire his silk draperies, exquisite vases, and rare flowers.

But after the visitors toured the palace and gardens, they wanted to see more. "Don't let our trip end," they would say.

A fisherman heard these words. "I can show you the most beautiful thing in all of China," he would say.

He began taking visitors into the forest to see a beautiful nightingale that lived there. At first they would simply grumble at the sight of the gray bird.

"We walked out here for this?" they said.

But then the nightingale would open its mouth.

The nightingale's song was lovelier than anything the visitors ever heard.

The visitors returned home and told their friends about the bird's beautiful singing. More people came to visit the palace gardens. The nightingale became known as the most beautiful thing in all of China. Everyone had heard of this most remarkable bird.

Everyone, that is, except the emperor himself.

The emperor of China was an old man. He stayed inside his palace and knew nothing of the nightingale. One day he received a letter that came from the emperor of Japan.

"I have heard of your wonderful nightingale," the Japanese emperor wrote. "I will arrive in two days to admire this bird."

The emperor of China was puzzled. He summoned his prime minister. "Have you heard of this nightingale that is the most beautiful thing in all of China?" the emperor asked.

"No, Your Excellency." The prime minister scratched his chin. "Nightingales are quite plain birds."

"That may be," said the emperor. "But the emperor of Japan arrives in two days. He expects to see this nightingale. Search until you find it."

The prime minister quickly searched every inch of the palace, but he could not find the nightingale.

One day before the Japanese emperor arrived, the emperor of China still could not find the bird.

The next morning, the emperor of China summoned the prime minister.

"The emperor of Japan will be here today," he told him. "You must find this magnificent nightingale."

The prime minister trekked into the woods and was about to give up when he came upon the fisherman. The fisherman led him right to the nightingale. The prime minister marched into the palace with the bird in hand just as the Japanese emperor arrived.

"So this is the famous nightingale, the most beautiful thing in all of China," said the emperor of Japan. "I must say, he looks rather plain."

Suddenly, the nightingale opened his mouth. Out came the most beautiful song anyone had ever heard. The emperor of Japan was speechless. The emperor of China cried tears of joy. "I must find a way to thank you for allowing me to hear your nightingale's song," declared the emperor of Japan.

Day after day the nightingale's song filled the palace. People crowded in to hear beautiful music. Someone always said, "Too bad the plain nightingale doesn't look as lovely as he sounds."

The emperor heard these comments, which made him very angry. The nightingale's song brought him such joy. He was happier now than ever before. "I will not have people saying unkind words about the lovely nightingale," he said.

The emperor gave the bird a golden perch to sit on. When he adorned the precious nightingale with ribbons and jewels, the people were delighted.

"Now the bird looks almost as lovely as he sounds," they said.

Every day the nightingale sat on his golden perch, wearing his jewels and singing his song.

The emperor thought the little bird looked tired and a little sad. He invited the nightingale into his private chambers to sing to him at night. The nightingale perched on the emperor's bed and sang just for the emperor.

"Gold and ribbons and jewels do not enhance your lovely voice," said the emperor. "You are the most beautiful thing in all of China when you are yourself, singing your pure, sweet song."

The emperor drifted off to sleep each night to the sound of the nightingale's beautiful song. The bird was happy, too.

One day a present arrived from the emperor of Japan.

"I hope you enjoy this gift," wrote the Japanese emperor. "It is a small token compared to the great joy you gave me when you let me hear the nightingale."

Inside the package was a nightingale decorated with emeralds, sapphires, and rubies. On its back was a tiny silver key. When the emperor wound the key, the mechanical bird began to sing one of the nightingale's songs. The bird did not sound as lovely as the real nightingale, and it only sang one song. Still, the emperor was pleased. He ordered a second golden perch to be placed beside the first.

"Now you will get some rest," he told the nightingale.

The people were happy. "Finally! A nightingale that looks as lovely as it sounds," they said.

They didn't notice that the jeweled bird's song was not as sweet as the real nightingale's song. They asked to hear the new nightingale over and over. The people ignored the real nightingale, so he flew home to the forest.

Only one person noticed that the nightingale had gone— the emperor. He missed his friend deeply. "Perhaps it's for the best," the emperor said. "The nightingale is happier in the forest."

The people never grew tired of the mechanical bird's song, until one morning, with a loud twang and a pop, it stopped. The emperor shook the bird. The prime minister wriggled its key. The bird would not play. They called in the watchmaker.

"A spring has sprung," the watchmaker proclaimed. "I'll fix it, but you'll have to be careful. Only wind it on special occasions."

The emperor was sad. He missed his friend the real nightingale. Now even the mechanical bird would not sing. The emperor grew sick and weak. The prime minister and all the lords and ladies of the court tried everything, but nothing helped. The old fisherman heard of the emperor's illness and told the nightingale.

The nightingale flew straight to the emperor's chambers. He perched on his bed and began to sing his beautiful song. The emperor opened his eyes.

"You came back," whispered the emperor. Tears of joy streamed down his cheeks.

The nightingale sang a sweet song for the emperor. The two old friends visited late into the night. The emperor sat up in bed, and the color returned to his cheeks. The nightingale was happy that he could make the emperor well.

The nightingale loved the emperor because the emperor appreciated him just as he was. The emperor loved the nightingale because he was his companion.

The two friends never parted. As long as the emperor loved the nightingale for being himself, the nightingale gladly sang his precious melodies in the emperor's palace.

Hansel and Gretel

Illustrated by Susan Spellman
Adapted by Jane Jerrard

Long ago, a poor woodcutter lived with his family on the outskirts of the forest. He had two young children called Hansel and Gretel. The children's loving mother had died, and the stepmother did not like children.

When hard times came and even the rich had little, the woodcutter's family had nothing at all. At last the woodcutter said, "How can we feed our poor children when there isn't even enough for ourselves?"

His wife answered, "Well, we must take the children into the woods and leave them there to take care of themselves. That way, maybe we will all have a chance. Otherwise, all four of us will starve to death."

Hansel heard his parents talking. When he told Gretel what he had heard, she cried.

"How can we manage alone in the woods?" she cried to her brother.

"Hush, Gretel," said Hansel. "We will think of something." That night Hansel waited quietly until his parents were asleep. Then he crept carefully out of the house and filled his pockets with white stones.

The next morning the parents woke up the children and told them they had to come with them deep into the forest to gather wood. The stepmother handed them each a small piece of bread to nibble on, and off they went. Hansel lagged behind, dropping stones on the ground from time to time.

When the family was deep in the forest, the father started a fire to keep the children warm throughout the night.

"Eat your bread and then lie down by the warm fire," said the stepmother. "We will be back soon, after we have cut the wood."

The children were so tired that they fell fast asleep after they ate. When they awoke, they were alone in the dark.

"How will we ever get out of this forest?" cried Gretel. But Hansel told her that when the moon came up they would find their way home. Sure enough, the bright moon shining on the white stones pointed them toward the path back home.

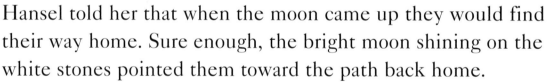

The tired children reached their cottage at daybreak. Their father was very happy to see them. He had sold the firewood for a good price, so for a while there was enough to eat.

But hard times soon came again. One morning, the children were again led into the forest with only a crust of bread.

"Don't worry, Gretel," said Hansel. "I have left a trail of breadcrumbs so we can find our way back."

Hansel and Gretel slept until the moon rose and then set out to find the trail. But alas, the hungry birds of the forest had eaten up every crumb. The poor children were truly lost in the forest.

Hansel and Gretel walked all night and all the next day. When they awoke from sleep the third day, they were almost too weak to walk anymore.

Gretel looked up and saw a beautiful white bird sitting on a branch. The bird sang a comforting song to the children, and then it flew on ahead.

The children followed the white bird to an amazing little house made of gingerbread and candy. The hungry children broke off a piece of the house and began to eat. Their mouths were full of food when they heard a sweet and gentle voice:

Nibble, nibble, like a mouse.
Who is nibbling at my house?

The door opened and an old woman hobbled out. She came along slowly because she could not see very well.

The children were very frightened, but the old woman said, "You poor, hungry children. You must be starving! But you do not have to eat pieces of my old house. Come inside and I will give you better food."

The old woman gave Hansel and Gretel a large, filling meal of pancakes and apples and milk. They had never before seen so much food on one table! Hansel and Gretel ate happily. Then the kind old woman put them to sleep in soft beds with warm, soft covers.

As Hansel and Gretel slept soundly, their bellies full with all sorts of delicious sweets from the old woman's gingerbread house, the old woman prepared more food for them.

She made apple dumplings, cakes, and pies for the two poor children, and as she baked these treats, the old woman grinned and hummed to herself. When she looked at the sleeping children, the old woman chuckled out loud.

Hansel and Gretel never guessed that the woman who seemed so nice was truly very wicked. She had built her house of cakes and candies just to attract children so she could eat them for dinner!

The old woman dragged Hansel to a wooden cage and locked him in. Then she woke up Gretel.

"Fetch some water and dumplings for your brother," she told the girl. "Fatten him up for me to eat!"

Gretel began to cry. The wicked old woman ignored Gretel's tears and made her cook and clean all day long.

Every morning the old woman told Hansel to hold out his finger so she could feel how fat he was growing. But Hansel knew that the old woman could not see well, so he held out an old bone for her to feel. This made her believe that Hansel was still too thin to eat.

After four weeks Hansel did not seem to be any fatter. But the old woman decided to eat him anyway and to eat Gretel as well.

The old woman told Gretel to climb into the big oven to see if it was hot enough to bake bread. But Gretel, who knew better than to get into the oven, said she did not know how.

"Foolish little girl," said the wicked old woman. She leaned into the oven to show Gretel how to get inside. Gretel knew just what to do. She gave the old woman a big shove that sent her all the way into the back of the oven. Then Gretel shut the oven door and ran to free Hansel.

"Hansel, we're saved! The mean old woman is dead!" cried Gretel. She unlocked Hansel's cage.

Then the two children stuffed their pockets with jewels they found in the house. They also took as much food as they could carry for their journey.

After hours of walking, Hansel and Gretel came to a lake. Gretel called to a white swan, who agreed to take the two children across on its back.

On the other side, Hansel and Gretel found the path for home. When they saw their own house and their father, they ran to him.

Their father could not believe his eyes!

The poor woodcutter laughed and cried with joy to see his children again. He had been very sad since his evil wife had made him leave them in the forest. After his wife died, he searched for the children day and night.

The jewels would buy food for the rest of their days. Their worries were over. They lived happily ever after.

The Selfish Giant

Illustrated by Sherry Neidigh
Adapted by Mary Rowitz

Every day after school, a group of children who lived near an empty castle played in its enchanted garden.

The garden was enchanted because it was summer there all year long. The trees in the enchanted garden never lost their leaves, the flowers bloomed all year, and the weather never got cold. Sometimes it rained, but only at night, when the children were sleeping soundly in their beds. It was always sunny come morning.

The children skipped rope, swung from the trees, and played games in the enchanted garden. When they got hungry, they plucked fruit from the trees and ate it.

The empty castle did not stay empty for long. It belonged to a giant who had been away for many years. One day he returned home hoping to find some peace and quiet after his long trip.

Instead, he heard the sound of laughter in his garden. He looked over the garden wall and did not like what he saw. There were children playing all sorts of games and eating the fruit from his trees.

"What are you children doing here?" the giant shouted. "This is my garden!" He chased the children away.

The children did not understand why the giant wanted them to leave. They were very frightened and ran away as fast as their legs could carry them.

Once the children were gone, the giant looked around the empty garden and smiled. Finally, he would have some peace and quiet. "No noise, no children running around," he growled to himself. He was a very, very selfish giant.

The children no longer had a place to play, no place was like their enchanted garden. One day, they stopped outside the garden wall. One curious boy wanted to see the garden with his own eyes, so he peeked over the wall.

The boy gasped at what he saw. The leaves of the trees were turning orange and were falling to the ground. The grass was now thin and brown. The flowers had wilted, and the birds had flown away.

"What has happened to our wonderful garden? It looks like it is dying," said one child. All the children became sad. Their beautiful garden was no longer enchanted.

Soon the garden became a cold and lonely place.

One day, a flower poked its head through the ground. The giant hoped it would grow. Suddenly a strong gust of wind came and scared the flower back underground.

The giant sighed. He did not understand the changes in his garden. The other day the garden was warm and full of life, but now it was dull and cold.

"At least now I have peace and quiet," the giant said, "and I don't have to share any of my garden with anyone."

The giant was simply being his selfish self.

The passing months brought even more changes to the garden. Snow blanketed the ground, icicles hung from the walls of the castle, and cold winds ripped through the trees. Nobody would have played in the frozen garden, even if the giant had wanted them to.

The giant could not figure out why it was so cold inside the walls of his garden. He could see that it was no longer wintertime, and the rest of the countryside was warm, not covered with snow.

"Something is not right," the giant said. He began to wish for his beautiful garden and for the children who had made it such a happy place. For the first time, the giant felt lonely.

The sad children stopped outside the garden wishing they could play there again. One day, a stone wiggled loose and fell out of the wall. The hole it left was big enough to crawl through. The children looked at each other excitedly and crawled through the secret passage one by one.

When their feet touched the ground, the snow began to melt. The grass turned green, and the sun began to shine again. When the children touched the trees, green leaves appeared. The birds came back and sang.

The children were filled with joy to be back in the enchanted garden.

In a corner of the garden, icicles still hung from one tree. A little boy looked up at the tree sadly. He wanted to climb it, but he was too small to reach even the lowest branch.

The boy sat down under the tree and began to cry. Suddenly, he felt a huge pair of hands gently lift him up and set him on a branch. Instantly, the icicles began to melt. Soon tiny buds opened, and leaves sprouted all over the tree. It was spring again in the garden!

The surprised little boy turned to see the giant who had once roared with anger at the children. This time the giant smiled and patted the little boy on the head.

The boy flung his arms around the giant's neck and kissed him on the cheek. The giant's heart melted as quickly as the icicles. He was sorry he had been so terribly selfish. He had missed the children.

When the other children saw that they no longer had to fear the giant, they rushed over to him. The giant scooped them up one by one and gave them each a giant-size hug.

"Does this mean that we may play in your enchanted garden?" asked one child.

The giant now realized that the children brought the magic to his garden. "From now on this is your garden," the giant said. "You may come here to play whenever you wish."

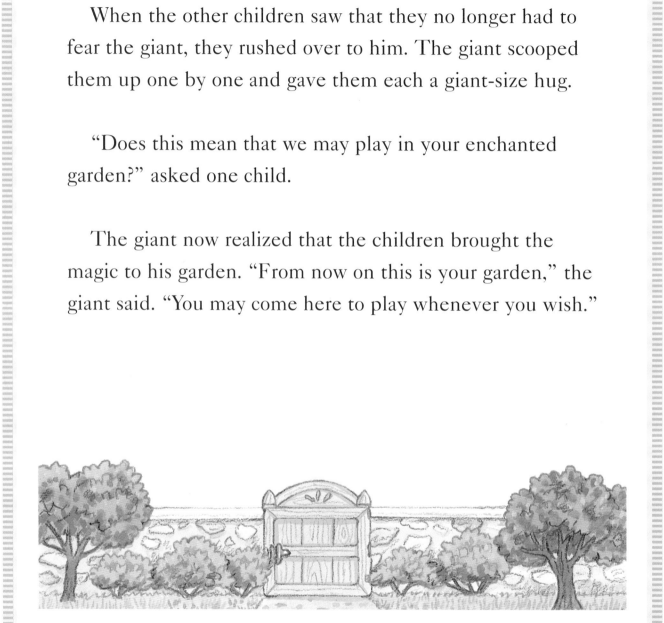

The Princess and the Pea

Illustrated by Anthony Lewis
Adapted by Eric Fein

L ong ago and far away there lived a lonely prince. He spent endless days traveling from kingdom to kingdom in hopes of finding a real princess to be his wife.

But every noble lady he met turned out to be unacceptable. It was not that the women were not beautiful or smart, for they were. It was that none of the women had those certain special qualities that made them real princesses. The prince would only marry a real princess.

The king and queen worried about their son and did their best to raise his spirits.

"I know!" said the king. "We will invite all the wonderful women from every kingdom to the palace for a festival."

The royal family held the festival as promised, and hundreds of young women came with the hopes of marrying the prince. But it was no use. The prince found something wrong with every one of them. They all returned home disappointed.

One night, a terrible storm fell over the kingdom. Thunder bellowed, and lightning lit up the sky for miles around. Among the few souls unfortunate enough to be caught in the downpour was a fair maiden on her way home. The young lady's carriage had lost a wheel.

"We shall seek shelter in that castle in the distance," the princess told her driver. "I'm sure they will help us."

They made their way to the castle through the rain and the mud. At the castle, the prince had been preparing for bed when he heard a knock at the door. Not being very sleepy, he thought he would answer the door himself.

"Forgive our intrusion, Your Highness," said the princess as she stood in the doorway dripping wet. "I am a princess. My carriage has lost its wheel. We have no place to stay."

Despite her muddy, rain-soaked appearance, the prince liked this young woman and wanted to help.

"Of course you may stay here," the prince said. "Come, allow me to show you to the fireplace, where you may warm yourself before you catch a cold."

"Thank you. That is very kind of you," said the princess.

Then the queen said, "While you warm yourself by the fire, I shall oversee the preparations for your stay in our guest room."

"You are all so good to me," said the princess.

The queen just smiled at her. She was skeptical as to whether the young lady was truly a princess. To find out, she devised a clever test.

The servants piled twenty mattresses, one on top of the other. Then they put twenty fine quilts, one over the other, on top of the twenty mattresses. So soft and lush was the bed that any ordinary person would sleep forever. But then the queen placed a small uncooked pea under the bottom mattress.

"If she is truly a princess, she'll get no comfort out of this bed. For only the delicate nature of a true princess will be able to feel the hardness of the pea under all these layers," said the queen.

The prince and the princess talked for quite a while before turning in for the night. They enjoyed each other's company very much and went to bed smiling.

When the princess arrived at the guest room, she saw the exquisite bed arranged for her to sleep in. The princess climbed into the tall bed and lay down. As soon as she did, she felt that something was not right. She turned onto her right side and then onto her left. It did not help. She tried lying on her stomach, but that did not help either. She even tried to sleep with her head on the opposite side of the bed, diagonally too. Nothing worked.

"Oh, dear," said the princess. "How will I sleep in such an uncomfortable bed?"

The next morning, the princess joined the royal family for breakfast. The queen asked her how she had slept.

"The bed was truly lovely and soft," she said. "But I could feel something hard underneath it. It had me tossing all night. You will not believe what I found underneath the bottom mattress–a pea!" said the princess, holding up the pea.

The queen whispered, "She is indeed a true princess."

The prince was happy, for he had fallen in love with the princess. He got down on one knee and proposed.

The princess agreed, for she had fallen in love with the prince, too. The prince and princess lived happily ever after.

George and the Dragon

Illustrated by Tammie Speer Lyon
Adapted by Brian Conway

This is the tale of St. George and the dragon. It has been told for over 15 centuries. It takes place during a time called the Dark Ages, when kings ruled the land, wizards cast spells, and monsters roamed free.

The queen of fairies had taken young George in as a baby. The fairies raised the child to grow up brave, strong, calm, courteous, quick, and clever. They taught him to be a noble knight.

At last the time came when George was old enough to seek out his destiny. The queen of fairies called him to see her.

"Your journey starts today," she told him. "You have many adventures ahead. Your quest will take six years."

The queen of the fairies spoke kindly to young George. "The world is filled with monsters and battles. You'll meet kings, paupers, wizards and witches, evil princes and kind princesses," she said.

George was sad to leave the land of the fairies, but he was not afraid.

"Always remember one thing," the queen added, tapping George's silver battle helmet. "Your greatest weapon, George, is your brain."

Then George set off. He traveled for weeks. As he approached Silene, he noticed the land changed from lush and green to dark and desolate.

It seemed the ground had been crossed by fire. There was no grass, only the darkest mud. The trees were bare and black, and a foul stench filled the air.

As George walked through this stark land, he did not see a living thing. Then George finally saw a castle in the distance. A high, solid wall enclosed the castle and the small city around it. The gate was closed up tight.

When he got closer, he saw a young lady. She crept quietly through the gate and up to George.

"Have you no sense?" she asked. "You would do well to leave here now and never return."

"But I am a brave knight here to help you," George whispered.

"Alas, sir," the woman replied, "you are but one man. I fear that you cannot help."

George looked at her and said, "It is my destiny. I will do all I can, even if it costs me my life."

"I am Princess Sabra," she said. "Come with me." Sabra explained why the kingdom lived in such fear. A fearful dragon had lived in the kingdom for many years, she told him. The horrible beast had ravaged the land and eaten all the animals.

Princess Sabra told George that the people had moved within the castle walls for protection. But soon the dragon had run out of animals to eat. The dragon had promised to come through the castle walls for his breakfast when the animals were gone, she told him.

"We gave up our last two sheep this very morning," said the princess. "Tomorrow we shall all perish."

"Then my timing is perfect," said George.

They came to a cave in the dark forest where a wise old hermit lived. Sabra and George crept up to the old hermit, who stared into his fire. He did not turn to look at them.

Suddenly the hermit spoke. "Long ago, it was told, two brave knights would come to know, the only way to save the rest: The Serpent's weakness is in his breath," said the hermit.

With those words, an ancient hourglass appeared at their feet. George did not understand. He asked the strange man, but the hermit would speak no more.

When George and Sabra left the cave, it was already dark. They knew they must hurry to the dragon's lair. They had to get there while the dragon slept. It was their only chance.

"The hermit speaks in puzzles," Sabra sighed. "What do we do with this ancient timepiece?"

George remembered that the queen of fairies had told him his best weapon was his brain. He studied the hourglass. "The hourglass will lead us," George whispered. "We must wait until all the sand has dropped through"

The smell as they approached the lair was horrible. George and the princess used George's shield to protect themselves from the dragon's fiery snores.

Suddenly the dragon stirred. The dragon raised up and rubbed his eyes. George watched the dragon rise and the very last grain of sand dropped through the hourglass. At that moment, the dragon yawned a great, fiery yawn.

"Now, George!" Sabra shouted.

George threw the hourglass into the dragon's mouth.

The hourglass broke apart on the dragon's tongue in a cloud of icy mist.

The dragon was really angry now. It looked down to see George and Sabra duck behind the shield. The dragon reared back to hurl a fiery blast at them, but only soft snow came from its mouth. The dragon took a deep breath and tried again, but its mouth shut tight with ice. The dragon jumped into the deep, warm lake to keep from freezing from the inside out.

That dragon never bothered another soul. Some have seen him coming up for air on occasion, but only on very warm nights. The dragon would not dare stay out of the warm water too long, for fear of becoming a giant icy statue.

George and Sabra had saved the kingdom. It was Sabra who was the second knight that the old Hermit had spoke of in his strange riddle.

The two arrived at the castle to cries of joy and triumph. The grateful people of Silene were no longer prisoners in their own kingdom.

The king offered George all he had in thanks, but George wanted no payment for his deeds.

"I have more adventures left to face," George told the people. "They are my greatest reward."

George shared the story of the dragon of Silene to anyone who asked along his journey. And it is still told today as an example of bravery.

Sleeping Beauty

Illustrated by Burgandy Nilles
Adapted by Jane Jerrard

Once upon a time in a far-off land, there lived a good king and queen who wanted a child more than anything in the world. At last, after many years, the queen gave birth to a beautiful daughter.

The king invited all the people in the kingdom to a great party to celebrate the birth of the princess. The queen asked seven fairies to be the baby girl's godmothers.

When the day of the party arrived, the fairy godmothers were the first guests to enter. The fairies sat down at a fine table at the head of the room. Each fairy godmother had a place setting with golden plates and cups decorated with diamonds and rubies. They were special guests.

But there was another fairy—a very old and unhappy fairy— whom the queen had forgotten to invite.

As all the guests sat down, this old fairy appeared. She was angry at having been forgotten, so the queen apologized and quickly set another place for her among the other fairies. But there were no more golden plates or jeweled cups. The old fairy had to eat off china and sip from crystal. This made her angrier.

As dinner was served, the fairies talked excitedly among themselves about their gifts for the princess.

But the evil old fairy did not join in their conversations. She only grumbled to herself. The beautiful young fairy who sat beside her at the table heard the old woman muttering to herself. The young fairy decided to hide behind the curtains in case the old fairy caused some mischief.

Finally the time came for the godmothers to give their gifts. While the king and queen sat proudly nearby, each fairy in turn stepped up to the cradle where the baby slept. Each fairy gave the child a magical gift.

"I give this child beauty," said the first fairy godmother.

"She shall be as good as she is lovely," said the second fairy.

"She shall have happiness all her days," offered the third.

The princess was also given gifts of a quick mind, dancing feet, and a lovely voice.

Then the old fairy stepped forward. She was still angry at the queen. "I curse this princess. On her sixteenth birthday she will prick her finger on the spindle of a spinning wheel and die."

Just as the queen was about to cry, the seventh fairy quietly stepped out from her hiding place. She was the youngest and kindest of the fairies, but her magic was not yet as strong as the magic of the other fairies. She could not reverse the evil fairy's curse.

"I cannot take away this curse," she said sadly, "but I can change it. The princess will not die when she pricks her finger. Instead she will fall into a deep sleep until a prince's kiss awakes her."

The king and queen thanked the young fairy, but they were grief-stricken and found little comfort in her gift. In the years before her sixteenth birthday, they did everything they could to prevent the curse from being fulfilled. The king ordered all the spinning wheels in his kingdom to be destroyed to try to save his little daughter.

As the years went by, the princess grew into a beautiful girl, blessed with all her fairy godmothers' gifts. It had been so long since the royal banquet that many people in the kingdom had forgotten about the curse.

Finally the day of the princess's sixteenth birthday arrived. In the morning, she decided to explore some of the towers in the castle, where she had never been.

At the top of the tallest tower, she came upon a room where an old woman sat at a spinning wheel. The young princess had never seen a spinning wheel, since they had not been allowed in the kingdom in her lifetime. The princess asked the old woman what she was doing.

"I am spinning, my dear," replied the woman.

"How clever!" said the girl. "Please let me try."

The old woman eagerly got up from the stool, and helped the princess sit down. But as soon as the princess started to spin, she pricked her finger on the spindle. Immediately she fell into a deep, deep sleep.

No one in the kingdom could wake the sleeping beauty. With great sadness in their hearts, the king and queen dressed her in a fine white gown and laid her in her royal bed. They surrounded her with silk pillows and blankets and brought her fresh flowers every day.

When the seventh fairy heard that the curse had come to pass, she quickly flew to the kingdom to help. She knew that the king and queen would be sad to watch their daughter sleep the rest of their days. She also knew that the king and queen could not help the sleeping princess.

The little fairy decided to cast a magical spell over the whole kingdom. Everyone in the kingdom fell fast asleep and would not awaken until the princess opened her eyes.

Last of all, the fairy grew a magical forest of thorny trees around the castle to protect it.

As the years passed, the people in the nearby countryside forgot the kingdom hidden in the thorny woods. Only a few of the older people remembered the story of the sleeping beauty.

Then one day a young prince was out riding over the hills exploring the countryside. He came upon the dark, thorny woods and wondered why it was so silent. Finally, he noticed a tower rising above the trees.

"What is that castle I see in the woods?" he asked some people in a nearby village. A very old man told the prince a tale that his father had told him about the hidden castle. It was the story of the sleeping beauty.

The prince grew very excited upon hearing this tale and decided to rescue the beautiful princess. He was prepared to cut his way through the thorny forest to reach her, but the trees parted magically to make a path for him—a path right to the castle door!

The prince entered the castle. It was very quiet inside. In every room he looked, he saw people sleeping soundly.

He searched through the entire enchanted castle before he found the princess in her golden bed.

The prince leaned down
and kissed her cheek.

The princess opened
her eyes. When she saw
the handsome young man,
she smiled and asked, "Is
it you, my prince?"

The prince was charmed
at the sound of her voice
and told her that, indeed,
he had come to save her.
Then he told her that he loved her already.

The prince and princess were interrupted by a great cheer.
The whole castle was awake! The king and queen thanked
the young prince for breaking the spell. They were grateful
to see their beautiful daughter again.

The king called for a great celebration which lasted for many days and many nights. Since they had just awoken from a long sleep, they had no trouble staying awake.

At the end of the party, the beautiful princess and prince were married in the palace. Their life together was happier than they had ever dreamed possible.

The Elves and the Shoemaker

Illustrated by Kristen Goeters
Adapted by Jennifer Boudart

There once was a shoemaker who enjoyed his work very much and set up his shop inside his small house. Times were hard for the shoemaker and his wife.

One winter, snowstorms kept everyone indoors. No one could buy any shoes. The shoemaker had little money for food and only enough leather to make one more pair of shoes.

His wife asked, "What are we to do? The cupboards are bare, and we have no firewood. Even our last candle has almost burned out." Her voice was gentle. She knew her dear husband worked hard.

"We must not worry," said the shoemaker. "Things will work out for us. I will finish these shoes tomorrow, and someone will buy them."

He cut out the leather and then went to bed. The shoemaker would finish working first thing in the morning.

When the shoemaker woke up early the next morning, the whole house was cold. He shivered and was very tired. When he got to his workbench, the shoemaker thought he would find the pieces of leather just as he had left them. What he saw instead was a finished pair of shoes! The kind shoemaker was amazed.

The shoemaker ran his hands over the shoes. Sure enough, they were made from the same leather that he had cut the previous night. The shoes were very beautiful! He could not have made better shoes himself. The shoemaker called for his wife to come and look at the wonderful shoes. She was just as amazed as he was.

The couple did not know who had given them such a wonderful gift. They did know that the shoes were worth a lot of money.

"What a great day," said the shoemaker. "We have a pair of shoes to sell, and the weather is finally clear."

At that moment there was a knock on the door. It was a traveler who had seen the shoemaker's sign.

"I work for the king," he explained, "and I have been traveling in the countryside. I have worn holes in my shoes. I need a new pair."

The traveler tried on the new shoes, and they fit perfectly! He walked around the shop for a few moments and said, "These are the most comfortable shoes I've ever worn." Then he gave the shoemaker a shiny gold coin to pay for them.

With the gold coin the shoemaker had enough to buy food, firewood, and leather to make two pairs of shoes.

The shoemaker also bought a wool shawl for his wife. The couple was very thankful for their good luck, and they decided they would work harder than ever to keep it.

Once again the shoemaker cut the leather into pieces ready for sewing and put them on his workbench. The next morning he found two more pairs of finished shoes, and they were just as good as the first pair!

Within hours the shoemaker sold both pairs of shoes and bought more leather.

The next day there were four pairs of shoes waiting on the workbench. This continued for many nights, until the shoemaker's shelves were filled with shoes like no one had ever seen before! The shoemaker and his wife could not believe their good fortune.

Life changed for the shoemaker. Now he and his wife always had wood for the fire and food to eat. The shoemaker bought better tools, lots of leather, and fancy brass buckles. He bought his wife a soft, new blanket and a lace cap.

The shoemaker was always kind to those who traveled from all over the kingdom to buy his shoes. He never charged high prices, but just enough to live a comfortable life.

Word of the shoemaker's fine shoes made him the most popular shoemaker in the land. He was very happy that his small shop was always filled with people, but something still bothered the shoemaker.

One evening he said to his wife, "Every night, while we are tucked in our beds, someone is working hard to help us. It's a shame we don't even know who it is. Why don't we stay up to find out?"

That night the shoemaker cut the leather into pieces and put them on his workbench. Like always, he turned down the oil lamp and left the room. But instead of going to bed, he and his wife hid in the doorway.

The moon rose and filled the room with silver light. Soon something was moving on the workbench. Two elves appeared! They were no taller than the shoe they were sewing. The elves quickly began to work, helping each other handle the leather and tools.

The elves' clothing was old and worn, which made the shoemaker and his wife sad. They were making shoes, but they did not have any for themselves. The couple tiptoed off to bed, leaving the elves to their work.

The next morning the shoemaker and his wife looked at the newly made shoes that were on the workbench, and they thought about the elves.

"Did you see how quickly those elves worked and how carefully they placed each stitch?" asked the shoemaker.

His wife answered, "I only saw their poor clothing and bare feet. I have an idea! We will make those little elves the clothes they need!"

"They are so tiny that it will be easy for me to make some fine shoes for them," said the shoemaker.

His wife clapped her hands. "Yes! And I will use a bit of my wool shawl and a corner from our blanket to make them tiny pants and coats," said the shoemaker's wife. The old couple started right away making the two suits of clothing for the helpful little elves.

That evening, instead of leaving pieces of leather on the bench, they left the tiny clothes and shoes. Again they hid behind the door and waited for the elves.

The elves appeared at midnight. They climbed upon the workbench then stopped in their tracks.

What was this? Where were the pieces of leather and the tools? The elves were amazed when they saw the clothes. At once they put on their fine new suits. They were so excited they began to sing:

What merry little elves are we!
These fine clothes fit us perfectly!
Who'd be so kind? We wish we knew!
We'd like to give our thanks to you!

The shoemaker and his wife were so pleased they could hardly keep themselves from cheering!

Weeks passed, and the shoemaker's shop was always filled with people. He still offered the finest shoes in the land, and people from all around wanted a pair.

One thing had changed, though. The elves had not come back since the night they received their new suits of clothes. The shoemaker and his wife did not mind. The shoemaker enjoyed his work and was happy to be back at his workbench. He and his wife were glad that they could help the elves who had worked so hard and had been so nice to them.

Three Golden Flowers

Illustrated by Marty Noble
Adapted by Lisa Harkrader

There once was a chief who ruled an island tribe. The chief, his family, and his tribe lived happily on the island, until one day the princess became sick. The chief called for the healers of the tribe. They gave the princess herbs, bathed her in oils, and burned spices to soothe her.

But the princess became more ill. She could barely lift her head from her pillow. A tribal wise man came to see the chief.

"Find three golden orchids," the wise man said. "Their scent will cure the princess instantly."

"Where are these golden flowers?" asked the chief.

"They grow only where the sun shines through the water," said the wise man.

The chief proclaimed that any man who could bring the three golden orchids could then marry the princess.

When the great warriors of the kingdom heard the chief's proclamation, they explored every inch of the island, but they could not find the three golden orchids.

On a nearby island lived a poor man, his wife, and their three sons. The sons were not great warriors. They were farmers like their father.

When the poor man and his family heard the chief's proclamation, they became very excited. They had explored their mountain forest searching for fruits and herbs to feed themselves when their crops failed. They knew exactly where to find the flowers that would cure the princess. Every year nine perfect orchids, delicate and golden, grew behind a waterfall in a hidden valley on the side of the mountain.

The oldest of the three brothers picked the three largest orchids. He placed them carefully in a basket and set off in his canoe across the sea.

When the oldest brother reached the island of the chief, he met an old fisherman on the beach.

"What have you there?" said the fisherman.

The oldest brother knew that everyone was searching for the three golden orchids. He was afraid the old man would steal the basket if he knew what treasure lay inside.

"Fishing worms," said the boy.

The fisherman smiled and let the boy continue on his way.

The oldest brother ran toward the chief's village. There he stood before the chief and opened his basket. But inside was nothing but worms, just as he had told the old fisherman.

The middle brother decided to try his luck. When he reached the island of the chief, he met the old fisherman.

The fisherman asked the middle brother the same question as the older brother. The middle brother was also suspicious, and his basket of flowers also changed to worms.

Now only three golden orchids remained. The youngest brother was determined to try. He picked the orchids and set off toward the island of the chief.

He met the old fisherman as soon as he reached the shore.

"What do you carry in your basket?" asked the fisherman.

The youngest boy was very honest. "I carry flowers that will cure the princess."

"Indeed you do," said the fisherman. He gave the boy a bamboo flute. "This will bring you all the luck you need."

The youngest brother thanked the fisherman for the flute, then ran to the village with the orchids.

At first the chief refused to see the boy. But the youngest brother opened his basket. Inside lay three golden orchids, as perfect as when he had first picked them.

The chief lifted them from the basket and arranged them on the princess's pillow. The princess moved her head. Her eyes opened. She looked up and smiled. She sat up to thank the youngest brother, and soon the princess and the boy were laughing and talking together.

The chief was glad his daughter was healthy, but he had expected one of his warriors to find the orchids. He did not want the princess to marry the son of a poor farmer.

"You've cured my daughter," he told the boy. "Now you must prove you are worthy to marry her. The princess keeps one hundred pet parrots. Take them into the forest tomorrow morning. Bring them back tomorrow night. If any parrots are missing, you will not marry my daughter."

The boy agreed, and the next morning he led the parrots into the forest. The birds flitted through the trees, this way and that. The boy spent the entire day chasing them, trying to keep them together. But by nightfall, he could not find one parrot.

Suddenly, he remembered the bamboo flute the fisherman had given him. He trilled a few notes. All the parrots flew toward him from the trees. The boy set out through the forest, and the parrots followed.

He returned to the chief's hut with all one hundred parrots.

The chief counted the birds. He counted them again. He called his advisors together, and they all counted the birds.

"One hundred parrots exactly," they all agreed.

The chief stopped and looked at the boy. He smiled, "You will make a fine husband for my daughter."

And so the poor farmer's son married the princess. He brought his parents and his brothers to the village. The boy, the princess, their families, and their tribe all lived happily together in their kingdom.

Three Little Pigs

Illustrated by Susan Spellman
Adapted by Jane Jerrard

One day a mother pig told her three little pigs that it was time for them to go out into the world to make their own way.

The first little pig met a man with a bundle of straw. The pig bought some straw to build a house. Soon a wolf knocked at his door and said, "Little pig! Little pig! Let me come in!"

"Not by the hair on my chinny chin chin!" squealed the pig inside his straw house.

"Then I'll huff, and I'll puff, and I'll blow your house in!" said the wolf.

The wolf huffed, and he puffed, and he blew the house in. He blew so hard that he blew the little pig away.

The second little pig bought sticks from the same man. Then he built his house with the sticks.

It was not long before the wolf came along. He knocked on the door, saying, "Little pig! Little pig! Let me come in!"

"Not by the hair on my chinny chin chin!" said the second little pig.

"Then I'll huff, and I'll puff, and I'll blow your house in!" threatened the wolf.

The wolf huffed, and he puffed, and he blew the house in. He blew so hard that he blew away the second little pig, too.

The third little pig met the same man. This pig bought a load of bricks. He built a very sturdy house.

Soon the wolf was pounding on his door, just like he did to the first two pigs. The wolf growled and said, "Little pig! Little pig! Let me come in!"

"Not by the hair on my chinny chin chin!" squealed the third little pig.

"Then I'll huff, and I'll puff, and I'll blow your house in!" roared the wolf.

The wolf huffed, and he puffed, and he huffed and puffed some more, but he could not blow that little pig's house in.

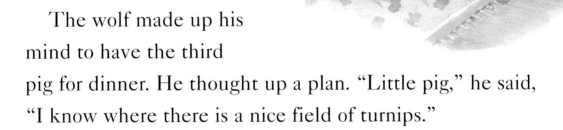

The wolf made up his mind to have the third pig for dinner. He thought up a plan. "Little pig," he said, "I know where there is a nice field of turnips."

"Where?" the little pig asked the wolf.

"At Farmer Brown's," he said. "I'll take you there at six o'clock tomorrow morning."

The little pig agreed. But he was too smart for the wolf. He got up at five o'clock in the morning, got the turnips, and was back in his house when the wolf arrived at six.

"Little pig, are you ready?" he asked.

"Ready!" scoffed the pig. "I've already gone and come back with lots of turnips!"

The wolf was very angry that he had been tricked, so he tried to trick the pig again.

"Little pig," he said sweetly, "I know where there is a tree full of juicy apples."

"Where?" asked the pig.

"In Granny Smith's garden," said the wolf. "I'll come for you tomorrow at five o'clock in the morning. We will go together."

The little pig woke up at four o'clock and went off to find the apples. The wolf also got up at four o'clock, but the pig was not home. The wolf went to the apple tree.

The little pig was just about to come down from the tree with some apples when he saw the wolf below.

The little pig was frightened. The wolf came close and called up the tree to him.

"My, you're up early," said the wolf. "How are the apples?"

The pig thought of a plan quickly. "Delicious!" he said. "Why don't you stand back, and I will throw one down to you."

So the wolf took a few steps back.

The little pig tossed the apple as far as he could. He threw the apple so far that he was able to scoot down the tree and run away. The little pig was safely home before the wolf found the apple he had thrown.

Back at his little brick house, the pig made applesauce and apple pie, and he still had plenty of apples left to eat. He was a smart little pig.

In the meantime, the wolf was furious that he had been tricked again. He thought he was trickier than any little pig, and this little pig had tricked him too many times already. So he thought and thought until he came up with another plan.

The next day the wolf went over to the little pig's house and said, "Little pig, there is a fair in town today. Let's go together! I'll come by for you at three this afternoon."

The little pig agreed, and you will not be surprised that the clever pig started out early for the fair. He enjoyed all the sights and sounds of the fair, but he did not stay too long. The little pig wanted to get home before the wolf showed up at the fair.

The little pig was on his way home with a big barrel he had bought at the fair when he saw the wolf coming up the hill toward him.

The tricky little pig crawled into the barrel to hide. When he did, the barrel started to roll down the hill!

The barrel rolled over and over, gathering speed on its way down the hill. The barrel with the little pig inside headed straight for the wolf. This frightened the wolf so much that he ran right home.

The wolf went to the little pig's house the next day.

"Little pig," he said, "I was going to meet you at the fair yesterday, when all at once the most frightening thing came rolling down the hill. I ran straight home!"

The little pig laughed. "Ha, ha! It was I that frightened you! I was in the barrel!"

The wolf was very angry when he learned that the little pig had frightened him with the barrel. He made up his mind right then and there that he would eat the little pig for his dinner that very day.

"Little pig," roared the wolf, "I am going to eat you for dinner today! I may not have been able to blow your house in, and I may not have been able to trick you, but I'm going to come down the chimney to get you now!"

With that the wolf leaped up on the roof. "Here I come, little pig!" he snarled down into the chimney.

But the smart little pig had hung a pot full of water over the fire. The wolf tumbled down the chimney right into the big pot of boiling water. The pig quickly put a heavy lid on the pot, and that was the end of the wolf.

The little pig lived happily ever after.

Little Dutch Boy

Illustrated by Linda Dockey Graves
Adapted by Sarah Toast

Long ago there was a boy named Hans who lived with his mother in a pretty town in Holland. The land of Holland is very flat, and much of it is below the level of the sea. The farmers there built big walls called dikes to keep the sea from flooding their farms. Hans knew that if a dike broke, the fields and town would be ruined.

One day Hans's mother packed a basket of food for Hans to take to their friend, Mr. Van Notten. Mr. Van Notten's house was outside of town, and it was a long way to walk.

As Hans set out, his mother told him not to stay too late. She wanted him to get home before it got dark.

Mr. Van Notten had only an old dog to keep him company, so he was very happy when Hans came to visit him. To get to Mr. Van Notten's home, Hans followed the main road out of town. The road ran alongside the dike.

Hans was very thirsty and hungry after his long walk, so Mr. Van Notten made cocoa and set out bread and cheese. After their meal, the boy and the old man talked by the fire.

When Mr. Van Notten's old dog scratched at the door to be let out, Hans noticed that the sky had become dark and stormy. He knew he should leave for home before it started to rain.

Hans walked quickly, but he was not even halfway home when the air became much colder and the wind began to blow very hard. Soon cold, stinging raindrops battered Hans as he struggled against the powerful wind. The weather made it difficult for Hans to walk, but he kept going. "If I just keep putting one foot in front of the other," said Hans to himself, "I'll be home soon."

The strong wind made the trees bend low, and it flattened the flowers. Hans was getting cold, and he had to hold his hat on his head to keep it from blowing away. "I hope my mother isn't upset when I arrive home so cold and wet," he thought.

Hans was getting more and more tired with every step, but he remembered that his mother wanted him home before dark.

Hans kept his head down against the wind as he trudged along the road. It was so dark that Hans had no idea he was nearing the town until he lifted his head. Hans was happy to see the dike in front of him. It meant he would be home soon.

Even through all the raindrops, Hans noticed some water where it should not have been. There was a small hole in the dike, and a trickle of water was seeping through.

Hans knew right away what must have happened. The storm whipped up the waves of the sea on the other side, and the pounding water made a crack in the dike.

"I must warn everybody that the dike has sprung a leak!" thought Hans.

Hans ran into town yelling, "The dike is breaking! Help! We've got to fix the dike!"

But no one heard Hans. Nobody else was outside, and all the houses had been completely shut because of the storm. All the doors were bolted tightly, every window closed and shuttered.

Hans realized his shouting was not doing any good. He stopped running to catch his breath. Hans tried to think of what to do next. His mother must be worrying about him, but he knew that the tiny hole in the dike was getting bigger every minute.

If the hole got big enough, the sea would break through the dike. All would be lost—the sea would flood the farms and wash away the pretty little town.

As fast as he could, Hans ran back to the place where he had seen the water seeping through the dike. Just as he thought, the crack was bigger now. Hans knew that the crack must be fixed soon. There was nothing else to do, so Hans balled up his fist and pushed it into the hole to stop the water.

Hans was proud that he could hold back the sea. He was sure that his worried mother would send people to look for him. But minutes turned into hours as Hans patiently stood there.

As darkness fell, Hans became very cold and tired, and his arm began to ache. He had to force himself to keep standing. To keep himself going, Hans thought about how important it was that he hold back the sea.

Hans thought about the warmth of the fireplace at home as he stood in the cold rain by the dike. Then he thought about how good it would feel to lie down in his snug bed. These thoughts helped the tired boy get through the night.

When Hans did not come home that evening, his mother began to worry. Even as the rain was falling, she kept looking out the door hoping Hans would come back. At last she decided that Hans must have waited out the storm at Mr. Van Notten's. She thought he must have spent the night there because it was too dark to come home after the storm.

After looking out the door one more time, Hans's mother closed up the house and went to bed, but she could not sleep. She was too worried about her little boy.

Early the next morning, Mr. Van Notten was walking to Hans's home. He wanted to thank Hans for the visit and thank his mother for the tasty food. When he came to where Hans was, the boy was trembling with cold. Hans's arm hurt from the effort of keeping his fist in the hole of the dike, and his legs were ready to collapse from standing all night. Still Hans had to hold firm for just a little longer while Mr. Van Notten ran into town to get help.

"Don't worry, Hans," said Mr. Van Notten. "I'll be back in a jiffy. You're doing a great job. Just hang on a little longer."

Soon Mr. Van Notten returned with someone to take care of Hans and materials to repair the dike. Hans was wrapped in blankets and carried home. He was put to bed and given warm broth to drink. His mother rubbed his fingers and his stiff legs.

Word spread through the town of how Hans had held back the sea all by himself. The townspeople were very curious. They went to the dike to see the hole that Hans had plugged.

As soon as Hans felt strong enough, he and his mother went to the dike to see the repairs that were being made.

Everyone in town was overjoyed to see Hans. They gave him gifts fit for a hero. They shook his hand and thanked him for holding back the sea. They thanked him for saving them from what would have been a terrible flood.

Hans was very proud. His mother was very proud of him, too.

The mayor of the town presented Hans with a medal to honor his dedication. All the townspeople cheered loudly. Hans would forever after be remembered as a hero.

Years later, after Hans was grown up, people still called him the little boy with the big heart.

The Ugly Duckling

Illustrated by Susan Spellman
Adapted by Sarah Toast

I t was a beautiful summer morning in the country. Beside a pond, a mother duck was sitting on her nest. She had been sitting for a long time, waiting for her eggs to hatch.

Finally the eggs began to crack. "Peep, peep," said the newly hatched ducklings.

"Quack, quack," said their mother. "You are the sweetest little yellow ducklings! Have you all hatched?" But the biggest egg had not hatched yet.

The tired mother duck sat down again on the last egg and waited. When the egg finally cracked, out tumbled a clumsy gray duckling.

This duckling was bigger than the others and very ugly. The mother duck looked at him.

The mother duck quacked to her babies to follow her. They all waddled to the barnyard. The gray one was a little clumsier than the rest.

"He's awfully big for his age," said a goose in the barnyard. "Why is he such a funny color?"

The gray duckling was frightened by the big goose. He stayed close to his mother.

The mother duck did not listen to the mean goose. She gathered up her ducklings and waddled off. "He does look different," she thought. "I wonder if he can swim."

The next day the sun shone brightly. The mother duck led all of her ducklings down to the pond.

"Quack, quack," she told them. "Do what I do."

One after the other, the eager ducklings hopped into the blue water. They bobbed and floated like little corks. They already knew how to paddle their legs and swim! All of the new ducklings swam very nicely, even the ugly one. The mother duck was very pleased. She decided to take her ducklings through the meadow.

"Follow me! Waddle this way and quack," said the mother duck.

The little ducklings did as their mother did. But the gray duckling was a little clumsy. He tripped on the tall meadow grass.

His own brothers and sisters started to laugh at the gray duckling!

"You look funny," they told him. "You walk funny, too!" They all laughed at the gray duckling.

How sad the ugly little duckling was!

At last the ugly duckling had enough and ran away. He came to a swamp where the wild geese lived. The tired little duckling stayed all night in the swamp.

In the morning, the wild geese found him. "You don't look like we do," the geese said to him, "but that's all right. You can stay here with us for now."

Just then a hunter's dog walked by, and the geese flew away. The scared duckling stayed still for as long as he could. When he knew the dog was gone, the little duckling set off across the meadow. Soon he came to a crooked little hut. The door was open just a crack, and in went the little duckling.

An old woman lived in the hut with her cat and her hen. She felt sorry for the ugly little duckling and let him stay.

The little duckling could not purr or lay eggs, so the cat and the hen picked on him day and night. They were very mean.

The teasing made the duckling miss the pond and bobbing up and down in the water, so he finally left the crooked little hut.

The duckling found a lake where he could dive to the bottom and pop back up again to float in the water. The wild ducks ignored him because he was so ugly.

Autumn came, and with it clouds and cold winds. One evening at sunset, a flock of beautiful, big birds with huge powerful wings flew overhead. Their feathers were shining white, and they had long, graceful necks. The sight of these swans, for that is what they were, made the ugly duckling wish that he could be so beautiful.

The weather got colder. It got so cold that one morning the duckling was stuck in the ice on the lake. Fortunately for him, a passing farmer freed him from the ice.

The farmer put the duckling under his arm and carried him home. The farmer's children were excited and wanted to play with the duckling. The duckling thought they were going to hurt him, and in his fright he ran right into a milk pail. Then he flapped into a bowl of butter and flopped into a barrel of flour. He made quite a mess!

The farmer's wife chased the ugly duckling out of the house and into the cold.

The children ran after the ugly duckling to catch him.

The duckling found a hiding place under some bushes. As the snow fell around him, he lay still until the children went indoors.

The ugly duckling had a very bad winter. Food was hard to find, and the frosty winds howled. When spring finally arrived, the warm sun shined, and a robin's song filled the air. The ugly duckling had survived.

Filled with the happiness of spring, the duckling spread his wings to fly. My, how strong and powerful his wings had become! The duckling flew over green gardens and orchards.

Then he saw three swans floating on a lake, and he felt a certain bond with them.

The ugly duckling wanted to be near the beautiful swans, even if they might be cruel. He landed on the water and swam toward them. When the three swans saw the duckling, they went to meet him.

As they drew near, the ugly duckling bowed his head to the water, expecting to be treated badly. Upon looking down, he saw that there was another beautiful swan floating gracefully on the lake.

It was his own reflection. He was no longer a clumsy, ugly bird. He was a swan!

His ugly gray feathers had dropped away as he grew over the long winter. Now he had shiny, white feathers, powerful wings, and a long, graceful neck!

"I'm beautiful, like you," he said to the other swans.

When he looked at the three swans, he felt a strong bond. They seemed to know how difficult it was to be clumsy, ugly ducklings, and they also seemed to share his newfound joy.

The swans made a circle around him and stroked him with their beaks. All that the young swan had gone through made this moment even happier. He saw the beauty of everything that surrounded him.

He ruffled his feathers and thought, "I never dreamed of such happiness when I was an ugly duckling."

As the years passed, the ugly duckling lived his life as a beautiful swan. He had babies of his own. He made sure that no one ever made his baby feel like an ugly duckling.

The Flying Prince

Illustrated by Kathi Ember
Adapted by Brian Conway

Prince Rashar lived in a distant land. He spent each day hunting and exploring the jungle. While hunting, Prince Rashar saw a large parrot land on a bush above him.

"I am the king of the parrots," it said proudly. "This is our kingdom, and you are not welcome here."

"I will not harm you," promised Prince Rashar. "How is it that you can talk?"

"Princess Saledra gave me that power so I can protect my subjects from hunters," answered the Parrot King. "She is our guardian. She's the nicest and loveliest princess in the world!"

"Where can I find her?" Prince Rashar asked.

"You could never find her," squawked the Parrot King. "She lives very far away in the city where night becomes day."

Prince Rashar thought of nothing but the princess for many days. He decided that he must find Princess Saledra. He took his bow and arrow and rode off into the jungle.

The prince traveled for four days. Suddenly, Prince Rashar heard angry shouts. He saw four trolls having a terrible argument.

"Excuse me," the prince said. "Perhaps I can help you."

"Our master left us these four magic things," the trolls answered. "But he did not tell us who gets what!"

There was a flying bed that would take its owner wherever he wished to go. There was a cloth bag that would give its holder anything he wished for. There was a bowl that filled with water upon command, and a stick tied to a rope, which could defeat and tie up even the strongest foes.

"I can help you decide fairly," said the clever prince. "I will shoot an arrow into the jungle. Whoever returns with the arrow shall keep the magic items."

The trolls agreed that the prince's plan was fair. So Prince Rashar shot an arrow into the air, and the trolls dashed into the jungle to find it. While they searched for the arrow, Prince Rashar took the magic items. He rolled out the bed and sat down on it.

"Bed, take me to the city where night becomes day," he said. "Take me to the city where Princess Saledra lives!"

The magic bed lifted the prince high above the jungle, then it zoomed through the air. At last the bed settled down at the gates of a distant city. Prince Rashar stopped an old woman to ask about Princess Saledra.

"Nobody sees the princess until nightfall," the woman said.

The prince was disappointed. He could not wait to see her. The old woman told the prince to go to the palace and wait.

The prince hurried to the palace. When the sun set, the city was dark for a moment. Then a door opened at the roof of the palace. Princess Saledra walked out from her room and stepped across the palace rooftop.

Her beauty shone more brightly than the moon. In an instant, night became day, and the princess was the reason. Prince Rashar could not take his eyes off her.

At that moment, he knew he loved the princess.

Prince Rashar took his bag of wishes and said, "Bag, give me a silk shawl, one that matches the princess's gown exactly." He reached into the bag to find a flowing silk shawl.

"Bed, take me to the room at the top of the palace, where Princess Saledra sleeps." The magic bed lifted the prince over the city. It landed on the palace roof, and the prince crept through the door to the princess's room.

The room was as bright as day, with not a lamp in sight. Princess Saledra was sleeping soundly in her bed. The prince set the shawl beside her bed. He stopped to gaze upon her beautiful face before he quietly left her bedroom.

The next morning, the princess awoke to find the beautiful shawl, as fine as the gown she wore. But her gown was one of a kind, spun with special silk. Princess Saledra was very curious about who her secret admirer might be.

"He must be a man of great courage," she guessed, "to sneak into my father's palace at night. And to make such a perfect shawl, he must have magic as strong as my own!"

That night, after the princess had fallen asleep, Prince Rashar ordered a very special gift for the princess. He ordered a diamond ring to match the princess's headband exactly.

The magic bed carried the prince to the palace roof. As he crept into the princess's room, she awoke with a start. At first, she was frightened, but then the prince explained who he was.

The princess saw that he was very handsome, and he spoke from his heart. Her heart softened further when she looked at his gift to her. The princess smiled the brightest smile ever seen. Prince Rashar and Princess Saledra fell in love instantly. They decided they must be married.

Each day, Prince Rashar and Princess Saledra flew over their kingdom on the magic bed.

Rumpelstiltskin

Illustrated by Burgandy Nilles
Adapted by Jane Jerrard

Once there was a poor miller who was in the habit of boasting to anyone who would listen of his daughter's great beauty and talents.

One day, on his way to deliver flour to the castle, the miller happened to meet the king. The miller immediately started bragging about his daughter. He told the king that she was the most beautiful and talented maiden in the land.

The king just yawned. The boastful miller was determined to have the king notice his daughter. So he bragged on. "Your Majesty, my daughter can also spin straw into pure gold!"

"Straw into gold?" said the king. "Now that is a talent."

The king was very greedy, so he ordered the miller to bring his daughter to the castle.

"If it is true what you say about your daughter," the king told the miller, "she will be very useful to me." The king rode off toward the castle.

The miller brought his daughter to the castle, and the king took the girl to a room filled with straw. He told his servants to bring in a spinning wheel.

"Now get to work," said the king. "If you do not spin this straw into gold by morning, you will die."

The poor girl knew how to spin flax and wool, but she could not spin straw into gold. She was so frightened that she began to cry. Suddenly the locked door flew open and there stood a strange little man.

"Good evening, pretty maid," he said. "Why are you crying so?"

The girl told the strange man that her father boasted to the king that she could spin straw into gold. But since she really could not, she must die.

The little man picked up a bit of straw. "What will you give me if I spin this straw for you?" he asked the maiden.

"I will give you my necklace," she replied.

The odd little man took the necklace and sat down at the wheel. He picked up straw and began to spin. By morning the spools held spun gold, and the man was gone.

When the greedy king entered the room in the morning, he was greatly pleased to see the gold. That evening the king took the maiden to a bigger room filled with even more straw. Once again he commanded her to spin all the straw into gold if she valued her life.

Locked in the room, the girl sat down and wept. Again, the strange little man appeared.

"What will you give me if I spin this straw into gold?" the strange little man asked.

"I will give you my ring," the poor girl replied.

So the little man took the ring, started the spinning wheel whirring, and by morning he had spun all the straw into bright gold. The king was still not satisfied. He sent the girl to a larger room filled to the ceiling with straw. Then he promised to marry her if she could spin that straw into gold.

That night the strange little man came for the third time and asked what the girl would give him if he helped her.

"I have nothing else to give you," she said.

"Then give me your firstborn child when you become queen," the little man replied.

As she did not know what the future held, the maiden agreed. By morning the room was filled with gold. The king married the miller's daughter, and she became queen.

By the time she gave birth to a beautiful child one year later, the queen had forgotten all about the strange little man.

But one day, he appeared while the baby was sleeping. "Now give me what you promised me the last time we met," he demanded.

The young queen was horrified. She loved her baby and could not give it up. "I'll give you anything else you want," she cried, "but do not take my child!"

The little man felt some pity for the queen, so he told her, "I will give you three days' time to guess my name. If you can guess it, you can keep your child."

The queen sat up all night making a long list of names. When the little man came to her the next day, she asked, "Is it Caspar, Melchior, or Balthazar?"

But for each one the man said, "No, that is not my name."

"Alex, Abraham, Aloysius? Boris, Bruce, or Brian? Casey, Chris, or Carlos?"

"No, no, and no again!" he answered with every name the queen read. As the strange little man left that day he called out, "Only two more days!"

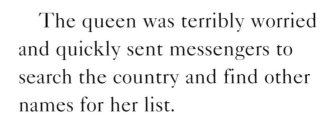

The queen was terribly worried and quickly sent messengers to search the country and find other names for her list.

When the messengers returned from their search, the queen wrote a new list of names. The second day she tried each one on the list.

"Could you be Ribcage, Muttonchop, or Lacelegs? Are you Hercules or Xerxes?" she asked.

"Of course not," said the little man.

When the odd little man left, the desperate queen sent for her messengers again. She ordered the messengers to search high and low for the little man's name.

As the last of the messengers was searching the forest, he came upon a little man dancing around a fire and singing, "Today I brew, and then I bake, and then the queen's own child I'll take. For little knows my royal dame that Rumpelstiltskin is my name!"

The messenger quickly ran back to the palace to report what he saw to the queen.

The queen cried out with joy and gave the messenger a large reward.

The queen prepared a final list of names for the little man, saving his own for last. When the smug little man returned later that day, the queen was ready.

"Is your name Kurt or Bert? Tom, Dick, or Harry?" asked the queen.

"No! Now give me the baby!" shouted the little man.

"Wait just a minute. I have one final guess," said the queen. "Is your name, by any chance, Rumpelstiltskin?"

The little man was completely amazed. He screamed, "How did you know it? There's no way you could've guessed it!"

The strange little man was so furious that he stamped his feet right through the floor and disappeared forever.

Little Red Riding Hood

Illustrated by Susan Spellman

Adapted by Jane Jarrard

There was once a little girl who lived in a small village at the edge of a very large forest. Everybody loved her.

Her grandmother, who lived in a house in the forest, loved the little girl most of all. The grandmother made her a lovely red velvet riding cloak with a hood. The little girl wore it every day, everywhere she went, so she became known as Little Red Riding Hood.

One day, while Little Red Riding Hood was out picking flowers, her mother called her to the house. She told Little Red Riding Hood that her grandmother was feeling ill. Little Red Riding Hood's mother was worried about the grandmother.

"We should do something to make your grandmother feel better," she told Little Red Riding Hood. "Leave your flowers and come inside to help me bake."

Little Red Riding Hood and her mother spent the day baking fresh breads and sweet cakes for Little Red Riding Hood's grandmother.

The morning after baking day, Little Red Riding Hood's mother said, "It would be very nice for Grandmother if you would take her these fresh breads and cakes." Little Red Riding Hood happily agreed and put on her hooded cloak.

"Be careful going through the woods," said her mother.

"You must stay on the path and walk quickly and quietly. Be careful not to drop the basket that you are carrying," said Mother.

"I will be very careful," promised Little Red Riding Hood, and she started down the path through the woods to her grandmother's house.

It was not long before Little Red Riding Hood met a wolf on the path. She did not know anything about hungry wolves, so she was not a bit afraid.

"Good morning," said the wolf. "Where are you going?"

"I'm going to my grandmother's little house," she answered.

"My grandmother lives under the three big oak trees," Little Red continued. "I'm taking her a basket of good food to make her feel better."

The wolf thought Little Red Riding Hood would make a tasty snack, but someone might come along the path any minute. So he slyly said he was going her way and asked if he could walk with her.

Little Red Riding Hood quickly walked along, as she had been told to do. The wolf thought of a plan.

"Just look at all those wildflowers at the side of the path!" he said. "Wouldn't it do your grandmother good to have a bouquet?"

The girl looked around her and saw the sunlight dancing on the flowers. Surely it could not hurt to take just one step off the path to pick a flower for Grandmother!

But one patch of flowers led to another, and soon Little Red Riding Hood had gone far from the path. She did not notice that the wolf was no longer waiting for her. The tricky wolf had gone on ahead to Grandmother's house.

Once there, the clever wolf knocked on Grandmother's cottage door.

"Who's there?" she called.

The sly wolf answered in a high voice, "It is Little Red Riding Hood. I have brought you a basket of goodies!"

"Lift the latch, child," said Grandmother. "I cannot get out of bed."

The wolf lifted the latch, leaped in, and frightened Grandmother right out of bed. She ran to the pantry and locked herself inside.

Then the wolf found Grandmother's lacy cap and nightgown. He put them on, climbed into her bed, and pulled the covers up to his wolfy chin. Then he waited.

By now, Little Red Riding Hood had picked a big, beautiful bouquet of flowers and found her way back to the path. She quickly walked the rest of the way to Grandmother's house and knocked on the door.

"Who's there?" called the wolf, as he tried to make his voice sound old.

"It is I, Grandmother," said Little Red Riding Hood. "I have nice things for you."

"Lift the latch, child," said the sneaky wolf.

So Little Red Riding Hood entered and cheerfully wished her grandmother a good morning. She put the flowers in a jug and the food on the table.

Grandmother looked so odd that Little Red Riding Hood felt frightened.

"Oh, Grandmother," she said. "What big ears you have!"

"The better to hear you with," said the sneaky wolf in Grandmother's voice.

"And Grandmother, what big eyes you have," said Little Red Riding Hood.

"The better to see you with," the wolf replied.

"But Grandmother, what big teeth you have," said Little Red Riding Hood.

"The better to eat you with!" cried the wolf as he jumped out of bed. As the wolf chased Little Red Riding Hood around and around the room, he tripped on the hem of Grandmother's long and lacy nightgown.

Despite his clumsiness, the wolf just about trapped Little Red Riding Hood in a corner. But as good luck would have it, that was the corner where Grandmother was hiding in the pantry.

At the right moment, Grandmother flung the door open with all her might and knocked the wolf off his feet. That gave Little Red Riding Hood a chance to run out the door and away from the house.

"Help! Help! The wolf is after me!" shouted Little Red.

As she ran down the path crying for help, a hunter heard her calls. He had been tracking this clever wolf for days and had noticed the paw prints leading to Grandmother's house.

As the angry wolf dashed out of the house after Little Red Riding Hood, the hunter took aim with his rifle. He fired one shot, and the wolf ran off into the forest.

At that, Little Red Riding Hood turned right around and ran back into the house to look for her grandmother. Inside, she found her leaning shakily against the pantry door.

Grandmother and Little Red Riding Hood invited the hunter in to thank him. They sat down to enjoy something warm to eat and drink, and soon Grandmother felt much better.

The hunter, Little Red, and Grandmother enjoyed the goodies that Little Red Riding Hood's mother baked.

As the kind hunter walked Little Red Riding Hood home, she said to herself that she would never go off the path again.

The Lion and the Mouse

Illustrated by Krista Brauckmann-Towns
Adapted by Sarah Toast

One day a lion was taking a nice nap in the warm sun. Nearby, a busy little mouse scurried about looking for berries, but all the berries were too high for her to reach.

Then the mouse spotted a lovely bunch of berries that she could reach by climbing the rock below them. When she did, the mouse discovered that she had not climbed a rock at all. She had climbed right on top of the lion's head!

The lion did not like to be bothered while he was sleeping. He awoke with a loud grumble.

"Who dares to tickle my head while I'm taking a nap?" roared the lion with a yawn.

The mouse could see how angry the lion was with her, so she jumped off his head and started to run away. The lion grabbed for the little mouse as quickly as he could, but she was too quick, and he just missed her.

The quick little mouse hurried to get away from the lion. She zigged and zagged through the grass, but the lion was always just one step behind.

At last the lion chased the mouse right back to where they had started. The poor little mouse was too tired to run anymore, and the lion scooped her up in his huge paw.

"Little mouse," roared the lion. "Don't you know that I am the king of the forest? Why did you wake me up from my pleasant nap by tickling my head?"

"I only wanted some lovely berries," said the mouse.

"Just see how much you like it when I tickle your head," said the lion.

"If you let me go, I am sure I will be able to help you some day," pleaded the mouse.

Suddenly, the lion began to smile, and then he began to laugh. "How could you, a tiny mouse, help the most powerful animal in the forest?" he chuckled. "That's so funny, I'll let you go—this time."

Then the lion laughed some more. He rolled over on his back, kicking and roaring with laughter. The mouse had to leap out of his way to avoid being crushed.

The mouse ran away, glad to be out of the lion's huge paws.

Still chuckling, the lion got up and realized he was hungry. He set out to find some lunch, and it was not long before he smelled food. As he walked toward the good smell, the lion was caught in a trap set by hunters.

The lion was stuck in the strong ropes, and the more he struggled, the tighter they held him. Fearing the hunters would soon return, the terrified lion roared for help.

"Somebody, please help me!" roared the lion.

The mouse heard the lion's roars from far away. At first she was a little afraid to go back, thinking the lion might hurt her. But the lion's cries for help made the mouse sad, and she remembered the promise she made to help him. The mouse hurried to where the lion was tangled in the trap.

"Oh, lion," said the mouse. "I know what it feels like to be caught. But you don't need to worry. I'll try to help you."

"I don't think there is anything you can do," said the lion. "I've pushed and pulled with all my might."

But then the mouse said, "Just hold still, and I'll get to work." She quickly began chewing through the ropes with her small, sharp teeth.

She worked and worked, and before long, the mouse had chewed through enough rope for the lion to get out of the trap!

"Mouse," he said, "I thank you for saving me, and I am sorry that I laughed at you before."

Then the lion scooped up the mouse and placed her on his head. He carried her back to the berry bush. "Mouse," he said, "I want you to reach up and pick one of those berries that you wanted earlier today."

The mouse plucked the biggest berry she could find. The lion took the mouse off of his head and held her in his paw.

"From now on, let's stick together," the lion said.

"Okay!" said the mouse, and they have been good friends ever since.

It just goes to show that you don't need to be as big as a lion to have a lion-sized heart. The little mouse kept his promise to help the lion. And the lion put aside his anger to help the mouse. Together they lived happily ever after as best friends.

The Goose Girl

Illustrated by Cindy Salans Rosenheim
Adapted by Lisa Harkrader

Once a princess named Elizabeth promised to marry a prince she had never met. The princess's mother, a kind and generous queen, prepared Elizabeth for her new home.

Elizabeth watched as her bags were loaded onto her horse, Falada. Falada loved the princess, and she loved him. Princess Elizabeth spoke to Falada and the horse spoke back.

"I'm afraid, Falada," said the princess. "What if I get to the kingdom, and the prince and the king don't think I'm worthy?"

"You are the most worthy person I know," said Falada. "The prince will be charmed by your kind heart and grace."

The queen chose a waiting woman named Zelda to look after the princess. Then the queen gave Elizabeth one last gift.

"This is my royal ring," said the queen. "When you arrive at your new castle, this ring will prove who you are."

Princess Elizabeth and Zelda set off. Elizabeth rode faithful Falada while Zelda rode a sure-footed old mare.

After a few miles, Princess Elizabeth was thirsty. She tried kneeling daintily by a stream, but she could not get close enough. So she sprawled on the bank of the stream and scooped water into her mouth.

As she drank, her mother's ring slid from her finger. Elizabeth did not notice that the ring had slipped off, but Zelda did. She waded into the stream and snatched it from the rock.

Elizabeth finished drinking and began brushing the mud from her gown. "Oh, no!" cried Elizabeth. "My mother's ring!"

Zelda held up the ring. "Is this what you're looking for?"

"Thank goodness! Zelda, you've saved me," said Elizabeth.

"This time, perhaps." Zelda slid the ring onto her own finger. "But what about next time? I should keep this for you. And after what just happened, I should take care of all your things. I'll ride Falada and keep an eye on your possessions."

"You're right," said the princess. "You're too good to me."

They switched clothes and horses. Princess Elizabeth and Zelda set off once more.

At the castle, the king and prince were waiting.

"Show me to my room and send up some food," said Zelda. "I'm tired and hungry."

The king was surprised by Zelda's rudeness, but he said politely, "We are delighted that you've arrived safely, princess." He turned to Elizabeth. "We'll find a room for you and send you a hot meal."

"Thank you," said Elizabeth. "But I'm the princess."

Zelda snorted. "You? Your clothes are rags and you were riding a swayback mare." Zelda held out her hand to show off the queen's ring. "This proves who I am. My mother gave it to me before we left."

The king sent Elizabeth off with the goose boy, Conrad. She was to be the new goose girl.

Each morning, Elizabeth and Conrad led the geese to a grassy meadow. Each night, Elizabeth slept on straw in the barn.

One day, Elizabeth found Falada in a pasture in the farthest corner of the kingdom. He was grazing by a fence.

"Falada!" called Elizabeth. "I've found you. How are you?"

"Fine," said Falada. "I'm exactly where a horse should be, but you are not where a princess should be."

Elizabeth and Falada talked and talked. Elizabeth insisted that she and Conrad take the geese to Falada's pasture each day. Conrad was annoyed and tired of trudging out to the far pasture each morning. He went to complain to the king.

"She talks to that horse all day," Conrad told the king.

"The horse talks back?" asked the king.

"Yes," said Conrad. "He tells her how broken-hearted the queen would be to see her daughter tending geese."

The curious king went to the pasture and discovered that Conrad spoke the truth. The goose girl was the true princess!

That night the king asked Zelda to help him with a problem. "A waiting woman has tried to pass herself off as a princess. Do you think forcing her to tend geese is the proper punishment?"

Zelda smiled. "No, your majesty. A girl like that belongs in the stable, cleaning up after the horses."

The king nodded. "You're quite right. And that is exactly where you shall go."

The king gave the ring to Elizabeth. "I apologize. I should have recognized a true princess by her goodness and grace, not by her fine clothes and jewels."

The Gingerbread Man

Illustrated by Tricia Zimic
Adapted by Priscilla I. Langhorn

One morning, before he went to work in his garden, an old man said to his wife, "Will you bake some gingerbread? I'd like gingerbread with my tea today."

The old woman decided to make a gingerbread man. She mixed the dough and cut out the cookie. She gave him two candy eyes, three candy buttons, and a sugary sweet smile. Then she popped the gingerbread man into the oven to bake.

When the woman opened the oven, the gingerbread man jumped out and quickly ran away!

"Run, run as fast as you can! You can't catch me, I'm the gingerbread man!" said the gingerbread man.

The old woman ran after the gingerbread man, but she could not catch him.

The gingerbread man ran through the garden, right past the old man working in the field.

"Stop, gingerbread man, stop! You are my teatime treat!" called the old man. But the gingerbread man did not stop.

"Run, run as fast as you can! You can't catch me, I'm the gingerbread man!" cried the gingerbread man.

The surprised old woman and old man chased after the gingerbread man, but the little cookie ran faster. He looked over his shoulder and laughed.

"Run, run as fast as you can! You can't catch me, I'm the gingerbread man!" laughed the gingerbread man.

He ran past a tomcat fishing in the pond.

"Stop, gingerbread man, stop! You look good enough to eat!" meowed the tomcat. But the gingerbread man just ran faster than ever.

"Run, run as fast as you can! You can't catch me, I'm the gingerbread man!" cried the gingerbread man.

The old woman, old man, and tomcat chased the gingerbread man through the field. But he ran much too fast for them to catch him.

The gingerbread man ran past a young calf.

"Stop, gingerbread man, stop! I want to get a taste of you!" mooed the calf. But the frisky gingerbread man ran faster!

"Run, run as fast as you can! You can't catch me, I'm the gingerbread man!" said the gingerbread man.

The old woman, old man, tomcat, and baby calf chased after the gingerbread man. But he ran on and on and on.

"Run, run as fast as you can! You can't catch me, I'm the gingerbread man!" cried the gingerbread man.

Next he ran past a pretty little white pony picking apples.

"Stop, gingerbread man, stop! I'd like to nibble those sweet candy buttons of yours!" said the pony. The gingerbread man kept right on running.

"Run, run as fast as you can! You can't catch me, I'm the gingerbread man!" yelled the gingerbread man.

The old woman, old man, tomcat, young calf, and pretty little pony ran after the gingerbread man.

"Run, run as fast as you can! You can't catch me, I'm the gingerbread man!" shouted the gingerbread man.

The gingerbread man ran past a big farm dog who was digging for bones.

"Stop, gingerbread man, stop! You'd make a fine dessert with my dinner!" barked the farm dog. The gingerbread man did not even slow down.

He said as he ran by, "Run, run as fast as you can! You can't catch me, I'm the gingerbread man!"

The old woman, old man, tomcat, young calf, pretty little pony, and big farm dog chased the gingerbread man.

"Run, run as fast as you can! You can't catch me, I'm the gingerbread man!" said the gingerbread man.

The gingerbread man ran past a mama duck gathering berries for her family.

"Stop, gingerbread man, stop! My ducklings would like you for a snack!" quacked the duck. The gingerbread man just laughed.

"Run, run as fast as you can! You can't catch me, I'm the gingerbread man!" laughed the gingerbread man.

The old woman, old man, tomcat, young calf, pretty little pony, big farm dog, and the mama duck chased the gingerbread man. But the gingerbread man ran faster and faster.

The gingerbread man ran past a busy beaver chopping down a tall fir tree.

"Stop, gingerbread man, stop! I want to eat you right now!" said the beaver. The gingerbread man did not slow down.

"Run, run as fast as you can! You can't catch me, I'm the gingerbread man!" said the gingerbread man.

The old woman, old man, tomcat, young calf, pretty little pony, big farm dog, mama duck, and busy beaver were far behind the gingerbread man.

They could not catch him!

The gingerbread man stopped at the bank of a wide stream where a fox was sunning himself.

"I'll help you cross this river, gingerbread man. Just hop on my back and I'll give you a ride," said the fox.

The gingerbread man hopped on the fox's back.

The fox said, "Watch out or you will get wet, gingerbread man. Climb onto my nose where you will be safe and dry."

The gingerbread man hopped onto the fox's nose. The fox opened his mouth wide and gobbled up the gingerbread man.

That was the end of the gingerbread man!

Little Red Hen

Illustrated by Linda Dockey Graves
Adapted by Jennifer Boudart

Little Red Hen lived on a farm with her five chicks. They lived a simple life and helped each other when there was work to be done. On the farm there also lived a dog, a cat, and a duck. They were all happy together. But when the time came to do the chores, the other animals never seemed to lend a helping hand.

One spring day, after sweeping the front path, Little Red Hen found some seeds and put them into a pail. She went to the field to plant them.

When she got there, Little Red Hen found the dog in his doghouse. He was sleeping soundly and dreaming.

"Who will help me plant these seeds?" asked Little Red Hen.

"Not I," said the dog as he yawned and stretched.

"Then I will do it myself," said Little Red Hen.

Little Red Hen began planting the seeds in a neat row. Before long, her five chicks came by.

"We will help you," chirped the chicks.

The chicks went to work with their mother. They scratched the ground with their feet and pecked out holes for the seeds.

By the end of the day, they had planted every last seed. After all their hard work, Little Red Hen and her chicks enjoyed the best night's sleep they ever had.

Several busy months passed for Little Red Hen and her chicks. Before they knew it, autumn had arrived.

After months of careful tending, the seeds they had planted in the spring grew into tall, slender stalks of wheat. Little Red Hen and her five chicks took their cart to the field to harvest the wheat.

When they got there, Little Red Hen and her chicks found the cat in the field. The cat was licking her paws.

"Who will help me harvest all this wheat?" asked Little Red Hen.

"Not I," said the cat as she swished her tail back and forth.

"Then I will do it myself," she said.

"We'll help you!" peeped her chicks.

Little Red Hen and the five little chicks harvested the wheat all by themselves. The cat sat by and watched. By the end of the day, they had a whole bundle of wheat.

The next day, Little Red Hen and her chicks took their wheat to the mill. Little Red Hen carried the bundle of wheat with her little chicks following close by.

Slowly, but surely, they got to the mill and gave their wheat to the miller to be made into flour.

Little Red Hen and her chicks brought the flour back to the farm, where they found the duck swimming in the pond. He was munching on some tasty weeds.

"Who will help me unload this flour?" asked Little Red Hen.

"Not I," said the duck.

"Then I will do it myself," said Little Red Hen.

"We'll help you," chirped the chicks.

Little Red Hen and her five chicks unloaded the flour, bag by bag, into the barn. It was hard work, but lots of fun. By the end of the day, they had unloaded all the bags.

In the morning, Little Red Hen and her chicks mixed some of the flour in a big bowl to make dough.

"Who will help me make the bread?" asked Little Red Hen.

"Not I," said the cat, the dog, and the duck together.

"Then I will make it myself," said Little Red Hen.

"We'll help you," peeped her five chicks.

They all took turns mixing the dough. Then they kneaded it into a loaf and put it into the oven to bake. Soon wonderful smells filled the kitchen.

Outside in the yard, the smell of the baking bread drifted over to the other animals. The dog, the cat, and the duck all came to the window of Little Red Hen's kitchen. The bread smelled so good!

Little Red Hen took the bread out of the oven and put it on the table. It looked as delicious as it smelled!

"Who will help me eat this bread?" asked Little Red Hen.

"We will!" said the dog, the cat, and the duck.

"Anyone who helped me plant seeds or harvest wheat or make dough can help me eat the bread," said Little Red Hen.

The dog, the cat, and the duck stood there sadly. But the chicks danced around! Then they ate the best bread they ever had!